Aloha, Penny,

I hope you enjoy!

Mahalo —

Birgitt
Van Wormer

Where the Honu Swim

A Novel

Birgitt Van Wormer

Where the Honu Swim

Prologue

The ocean sparkled in the bright sunlight. The verdant West Maui Mountains towered in the background, dark shadows deepening the crevices between the ridges. Four young volunteers walked slowly down the beach toward the water's edge, each one of them carefully holding onto a side of a massive honu's carapace. His three flippers were flapping furiously, his head stretched out eagerly toward the ocean. His front left flipper was missing. He had been found on the beach dehydrated and injured and had to undergo amputation surgery due to severe bilateral strangulation wounds caused by fishing line entanglement. After almost five months of rehabilitation including laser therapy, antibiotics, massage and topical wound care, he had now finally been cleared for release. The volunteers lowered him into the clear water and let go. He quickly dove down and disappeared in the waves, the onlookers all clapping happily as they caught one last glimpse of his carapace that now had a number etched into its side for recognition. The four volunteers high fived. Another honu had been rescued and released back into its ocean home.

Chapter 1

Mark Baldwin squinted into a ray of sunshine coming through the open strips of vertical blinds in the bedroom moments before the alarm went off.

A creature of habit, he always woke up a few seconds before the alarm. Stretching his arm, he turned the alarm off, hoping it wouldn't wake Sienna. Today was Saturday. He hated when he forgot to turn his alarm off on weekends. He jumped up and turned the plastic handle to close the blinds, then hopped back under the covers.

He hadn't been quiet enough. Sienna stirred. She pushed a strand of auburn hair out of her face and snuggled up against him. He lifted his arm, and she moved closer.

"Good morning," she said as she looked up into his speckled blue eyes and gave him a gentle kiss on the lips. They turned toward each other in a tight embrace, their legs intertwining, and kissed each other, breathing heavily.

Suddenly, the door was pushed open, and Lilly jumped onto the bed.

"Mark, can we go out in the boat today?" asked Lilly, bouncing up and down.

"Lilly, calm down, you're hurting me," said Sienna. She

grinned at Mark and sighed. Mark had a hard time keeping a straight face as well. With a total of four kids aged six to seventeen living with them, the days of undisturbed intimacy were over.

Lilly was too excited and wouldn't back off. She was determined to do something really cool this weekend.

"Come on, guys, you promised," insisted Lilly. "We haven't been out in the boat forever! And you guys are going to Maui without us and leaving us with Grandma and Grandpa, so you owe us!"

That was a sore subject.

A few weeks ago, Mark had received an email from his old friend Josh Templeton with the Turtle Rescue on the Hawaiian island Maui. Mark had worked there for a year right after college before starting his position at the Turtle Sanctuary in Turtle Key. He had developed a special non-invasive surgery procedure for the removal of tumors caused by fibropapillomatosis (FB). Josh wanted him to come to Maui for a few weeks, assist the local vets in treating FB and train them using his new treatment method. Unfortunately, FB occurred more and more in Hawaii due to worsening pollution.

Bridget, the Turtle Sanctuary's manager, and Sienna hated the idea of not having their best veterinarian around for a few weeks, but they couldn't say no. The Maui Turtle Rescue had helped them in the past as well. Sienna would miss Mark, but she was excited for him. She had organized a trip to Maui to visit him for a week, arriving a few days later since she had a few deadlines at work to take care of. She had never been to Hawaii, so this would be the opportunity of a lifetime. Thank goodness, the kids' grandparents could take care of Lilly, Lindsey and Leo for a while. Sydney could stay with her mom.

Mark was excited as well. He'd missed Maui and couldn't wait to go back for a visit.

Mark sat up and put on his round John Lennon glasses. He jumped out of bed wearing just a pair of thin pajama pants and pulled a t-shirt over his head. "Alright. How about breakfast first with some pancakes and my special key lime syrup?"

"Yes! My favorite!" Lilly followed him into the kitchen. Sienna sighed and looked at the time on her phone. Deciding it was way too early, she pulled the comforter back over her head. She couldn't fall back asleep with all the banging in the kitchen as Mark and Lilly got out bowls and dishes, made coffee and cut up fruit.

Mark explained how to make pancakes, counting out the ingredients as he added them to a bowl. Sydney, Mark's daughter from his previous marriage, joined them as well. Lilly and Sydney were put in charge of pouring the batter into the frying pan. Mark directed them patiently. It sounded like they were making quite a mess though. Sienna heard a lot of cleaning and less cheering.

One and a half years ago, her life was very different. She had been working as a lawyer in Boston when she received the horrible news that her sister and brother-in-law had been in a fatal car accident. She had traveled down to the Keys where she had grown up, the Turtle Sanctuary in Turtle Key, and given up her lucrative job as a lawyer to begin a new life raising her two orphaned nieces Lilly and Lindsey as well as her nephew Leo.

Things had been rough at times since she was single and had no idea how to raise a family. Meeting the man of her dreams, veterinarian Mark Baldwin, who also had a seven-year-old daughter and was a great dad, had awoken a deep-down familial need and desire in Sienna. He and Sienna had formed a patchwork family that mostly got along and had a lot of fun together.

Mark essentially lived with Sienna and the kids in the cottage behind the Turtle Sanctuary. Every other week they had Mark's daughter, Sydney, who was in the same class as Lilly at Stanley Switlik Elementary School. The two girls had become best friends. Sienna had settled in Turtle Key quite well. She worked one day a week for her friend Natalia's company, Pearls and Gems International in Key West as a freelancer for her old Boston firm from home (which turned into some long evenings) and from time to time for the Turtle Sanctuary when legal advice was needed.

From the bedroom, based on the girls' happy chatter and the aroma of pancakes, Sienna sensed breakfast was done. Even Lindsey and Leo awoke to the aroma wafting through the house.

Lilly and Sydney called up the stairs, "Breakfast!"

Sienna, freshly showered and dressed in casual boating clothes, stepped into the busy kitchen. She kissed Mark, poured herself a cup of coffee and sat at the table.

Sydney whined and begged Mark to take her on his upcoming trip to Maui.

"No, Dad, I don't want to stay with Mom for four weeks. She never lets me do anything."

"Sydney, sometimes we can't choose what we want when work is involved. I really don't have a choice, and I can't take you with me. You need to go to school."

Sydney's face lit up as she continued whining and pestering. "Oh, yeah, take me with you! I can home school for that time! I promise, I promise, I'll be good about doing all my work. P-leeeeease…"

"Sydney, I don't even know where I'm staying yet. I'm sure there's not enough space. And I'll be working and won't have time for you."

"Well, Sienna is going."

He was stumped for a moment.

Sienna had an idea. "How about we ask Sydney's mom if Sydney can stay with us for part of the time? I wouldn't mind having Sydney here; nor would Grandpa Richard and Grandma Rose when I'm gone. She has the same schedule as Lilly."

"Oh, yeah," exclaimed Lilly. "Please ask Sydney's mom if she can stay with us. Otherwise, I'll be totally lonely! Sienna gone, Mark gone and Sydney too!"

"Yeah, Dad, then I don't have to go to Maui if I can stay with Lilly. We can be innepenant."

"It's 'independent,'" Mark corrected her. "Okay, I'll ask your mom. I'm not sure what she'll say, but she might be okay with it."

Mark and Sienna exchanged glances. Mark's ex-wife, Isabel Baldwin, was a local police officer. She wasn't happy about her separation from Mark and was uncooperative whenever they asked her to switch weeks or do them other favors regarding

Sydney.

Mark handed Sienna a plate with two pancakes and some delicious key lime syrup. Famished, she grabbed some fruit that Mark had cut up and cleaned her plate in record time.

As soon as everyone finished eating, Sienna said, "Lets go, everyone."

"Can Alana come?" asked Leo. Alana was his girlfriend. "I made plans to hang out with her, and I can't just cancel."

Mark counted the children, Sienna and himself.

"No problem. We're six people, one more is fine. But tell her to hurry. We're leaving in twenty minutes at the latest. I need to take care of some things at the Turtle Sanctuary afterwards. And start packing."

He was running out of time.

Twenty minutes later, Mark's center console V-hull departed from the Turtle Sanctuary's dock with everyone on board. The smaller kids wore swim vests, and everyone looked out at the beautiful turquoise water. Mark started out slow because the entire area around the docks was a shallow no wake zone.

Sienna pointed at two pelicans taking off out of the mangroves. It looked like they were following them. As soon as the boat passed the buoy marking the no wake zone, Mark yelled, "Hold on, everyone," and put the boat in full throttle. The two outboard engines roared, and they shot across the water, full speed ahead toward the Seven Mile Bridge.

Everyone held on to the railing as the wind played with their hair, tossing and pulling it back. Every one of them loved the ocean and being out on a boat, and they enjoyed the ride.

Mark pointed at a pod of dolphins jumping in and out of the sparkling water.

Mark slowed down to minimum speed again to make his way underneath the Seven Mile Bridge pillars to the other side.

After a few minutes, they spotted the tall red-orange structure of Sombrero Key Light in the distance. They came here to their favorite snorkeling spot whenever they could. It never got old.

The lighthouse was located on a mostly submerged reef. The name Sombrero Key went back to the Spanish, and old charts showed a small island at the spot, but by the later 19th Century the island had eroded away with some parts of the reef exposed at low tide.

Other boats were already sprinkled around the lighthouse, but Mark easily found a spot and released the boat's anchor. Sienna and Mark made sure everyone applied reef-safe sunscreen and then lovingly rubbed it onto each other's backs, enjoying the gentle touches. They all donned their snorkel gear and jumped into the crystal-clear warm water.

The fish and ocean life were bountiful. A small school of rainbow parrotfish fed on brain coral. Electric yellow and blue angelfish and a big mean looking barracuda swam by, thankfully ignoring them. Hiding underneath some coral, they spotted a small octopus, and a moray eel quickly disappeared in a crack. Nothing was more fun and relaxing than watching the underwater world. They wished they could be fishes themselves and not have to come up for air.

After a while though, the exercise and salt water had tired them out, and they took a break in the boat. Mark opened a cooler and handed out snacks and sandwiches that he and Sienna had prepared before they left. They all sat and enjoyed the warm mid-November sun.

Mark gazed at Sierra's slender body in her tropical cut-out bathing suit. She smiled and gave him a tender kiss on the lips as she put her arm around him. Even though she loved the kids and spending time with them, sometimes she wished she and Mark had more privacy and time for themselves. But now she had something to look forward to: Maui.

Chapter 2

The final fasten-seatbelt *ding* and the captain's announcement about the upcoming landing came over the speakers. Just like most other passengers, Mark looked out the Boeing 787 window full of excitement. The intercom crackled. "This is your captain speaking. We'll be landing in about fifteen minutes. It's a balmy eighty degrees on this beautiful November day. Down below you'll see the North Shore and Kahului. In the distance is Haleakalā, House of the Sun, the massive dormant volcano, making up more than 75% of the island of Maui. The demigod Maui lassoed the sun, slowing its passage to give people a longer growing season."

Mark couldn't wait to take Sienna hiking to see the sunrise up on Haleakalā. Watching the sun rise at the ten-thousand-foot summit and the glowing lava fields below when the first rays of light appeared was a spiritual experience. As usual, the summit was covered in clouds.

Mark packed up his laptop and other belongings as the plane touched down in Kahului. He messaged Sienna that he had landed but was still on the plane. It was already 10 pm in Florida. Sienna would be asleep already, especially after taking Mark to the airport early in the morning.

Josh was waiting at baggage claim. They gave each other a big bear hug. Josh was an extremely tall and lanky man in his late thirties. His long curly blonde hair was tied back in a ponytail. His bright blue eyes sparkled like jewels, and laugh lines appeared in his tanned face as he smiled at his friend.

They had gone to the College of Veterinary Medicine at the University of Florida together, and Josh had gotten Mark the internship at the Maui Turtle Rescue years ago. They hadn't seen each other since Mark had moved to the Keys almost eleven years ago.

"Wow, you haven't changed at all, brah!" said Josh. "Looks like life has been treating you well!"

"My divorce was a little rough and turned my beard grey," Mark replied with a knowing look. Josh was currently going through a divorce himself. "But I'm happy again. I can't wait for you to meet Sienna."

"Too bad you got involved again," grinned Josh. "I would have made you move back here so we could enjoy life as two swingin' singles again." Josh clapped Mark on the back as he ushered him over to baggage claim.

"Sorry, I forgot to get you a lei," continued Josh. "But I have a hook up for you when Sienna gets here. The ladies love getting them."

Mark grinned. His friend's sense of humor hadn't changed a bit, and he knew they were going to have a great time together.

"Wait until you see my current pad. I'm house sitting for a friend who's in Europe for two months. I couldn't get out of Melanie's place soon enough. We were ready to kill each other, and it was getting unhealthy for the kids. The house is in Wailea in a neighborhood I could never afford. It even has its own pool."

"Is it okay with your friend if Sienna stays there too?"

"Yeah, brah, he's cool. He's a pro golfer. The only downside is that I'm watching his two young golden retrievers. They're nuts and need exercise twice a day. If I stay out late for a turtle rescue or something else, I need to hire a dog sitter."

"Sienna can help and walk them in the morning if she's not busy. We really appreciate you letting us stay with you. Condos and hotels are pricey on Maui."

"Yeah, they are. I'm going to have a hard time finding a house or condo close by with my salary. I'd love to stay close to the kids in Kihei."

"I'm so sorry about your divorce, it must be hard on the kids. You'll have to tell me about it."

"I'll tell you later over drinks," replied Josh.

Mark grabbed his suitcase when he spotted it on the baggage carousel. They walked toward an old gray SUV in the parking area. Josh opened the back hatch and Mark lifted his suitcase inside. They rolled their windows down, and Mark gazed out toward the glistening water on the drive to Wailea.

Josh took a left up a hill into a luxurious residential neighborhood. He passed some gorgeous new mansions and took a right into the driveway in the far back corner. It belonged to a big two-story cottage, older than the others, but, due to its patina and age, much more beautiful than all the modern McMansions. Its yard was a lush jungle while the others had manicured lawns with rather boring, albeit well-kempt, landscaping. Mark whistled as they stepped onto a spacious covered lanai. This was a beautiful perch to enjoy the trade winds and a bird's-eye view of the sunset.

"Wow, who did you say this pro golfer is?"

"It's Clark Lang. Last year's Masters champion."

Mark whistled. "How did you meet him?"

"My co-worker Kaipo and I saved him from drowning last year. We had just been notified about a honu in distress and were out in the boat. He was swimming far out in the ocean and had a bad cramp. We've been friends since. He's a nice guy. You should see the parties he throws here."

They took their shoes off, as was customary in Hawaii, and entered a large foyer and living area. High ceilings gave the home a sense of spaciousness. The floor-to-ceiling windows and sliding glass doors opened to a large deck in the back. Mark envisioned the parties Josh talked about.

Mark didn't have much time to marvel at the beautiful house because two rambunctious golden retrievers almost knocked him to the ground. Their tails wagged so hard they knocked a framed photo off a sideboard. They whined as they jumped up on the two men, as if they were appalled they had been left alone all day. Josh and Mark petted them for a few minutes until Josh opened the sliding glass door leading onto the deck and fenced-in back yard. The dogs followed him and disappeared outside. Josh sighed.

"Yeah, they're a bit crazy. They're still puppies and need a lot of exercise. Their names are Arnold Palmer and Ben Hogan."

"That's hilarious!"

Josh looked out a west-facing window, checking out how low the sun was. "How quickly can you be ready for dinner? Do you need a shower? Sunset is in about forty minutes. We could go down to Five Palms for dinner and a few drinks. My buddy Keanu can always squeeze us in. Remember that place? We'd better take advantage of it, they're closing this location soon. I think their lease wasn't renewed."

Mark remembered Five Palms very well, it had already been one of their favorite places to hang out eleven years ago. "Oh, that's too bad. Yeah, a quick shower would be great after that flight."

"Okay, let me show you your room," said Josh. "I'll feed the dogs and throw a few balls to tucker them out while you shower." He walked up a wooden staircase leading to an open loft on the second floor. Bookshelves covered an entire wall. A comfortable leather seating arrangement with several Hawaiian throws and quilts sat in the middle of the room. Paintings of tropical flowers covered the walls, and trophies were displayed in a glass case. Mark followed him, carefully carrying his suitcase to keep from scratching the expensive wood floors. Two wood doors with antique crystal doorknobs led off from the loft. Behind one of them was the room Mark and Sienna were going to use.

"Every room in the house has an ensuite bathroom," explained Josh as he walked ahead of Mark. He opened a door to one of the guest rooms and then a second door leading to a generous bathroom. "I'm ready whenever you are." Josh walked back downstairs, leaving Mark to get ready.

The bathroom sported an old clawfoot tub but also a

modern shower stall. It perfectly combined contemporary and antique design to maximize the users' comfort. Mark took his sweaty clothes off and stepped into the shower. Jets sprayed him from all sides. He stepped out after five minutes, refreshed and relaxed. With a towel wrapped around his hips, he walked over to his suitcase and got some nicer shirts out to hang up. Then he put on a pair of thin slacks and a button up shirt.

As they walked outside, Mark noticed the typical old Hawaiian style of the large fenced-in property. Majestic fruit trees, towering royal palms and a koi pond on the side of the house highlighted the landscape. As they drove out of the neighborhood, Mark looked at the other new houses and shook his head.

"What a shame, I'm sure these were all houses like your friend's before they were bulldozed to make room for these McMansions."

"Yeah, he did a sensible job refurbishing it. I think the house was in quite bad shape when he bought it. But it must have been a few million in this location."

At Five Palms, they walked all the way down to the water and entered the restaurant. The employees greeted Josh with high fives and fist bumps. The maître d', a handsome young local, stepped up and gave Josh a manly hug. "Hey, haven't seen you in a while, brah. Where've you been?"

"Just workin', brah," replied Josh. "Keanu, this is my old friend Mark. He's visiting from Florida and is going to be working with me at the Turtle Rescue for a few weeks."

"Aloha," they both said.

"Follow me, guys, I have a great table for you. The sun is

just setting."

Keanu led them to the nicest table in the restaurant on a patio surrounded by tall palm trees and blooming hibiscus overlooking Keawakapu Beach. He took the "Reserved" sign off, grinning at Josh. He always saved a good table for his regulars and friends.

"Shall we start you off with some mai tais?" They both nodded.

Stacey, one of the servers, brought them their drinks and menus and recited the day's specials. The fiery sun sank into the ocean, painting the sky shades of red, orange and purple. It was a spectacular sunset.

Josh lifted his glass and said, "Thanks for coming old buddy. Even if you weren't teaching us your new laser method, we can really use an additional vet right now."

Mark lifted his mai tai and clinked it with Josh's.

"Okole maluna. Bottom's up!" They both drank a big swig and smiled at each other. "How could I say no to a friend in need and a trip to paradise?"

"We have an unusual amount of injured honu since the turtle hospitals on Oahu and the Big Island closed. We got a honu from the Big Island the other day that was hit by a boat. The carapace is extremely damaged. There's a hole right in the middle of it at least eight inches wide."

"Poor guy."

"He's massive, almost two hundred pounds. I'd love your input on him, though I think we just need to wait until the tissue underneath the carapace grows back."

Mark nodded. "I'm sure you're right. There's probably not

much else that can be done except wait. Poor guy. I'll examine him tomorrow. I can't wait to see your facility. It sounds like it's grown a lot since I was here last."

"Yes, it's become quite the operation. We have about twenty honu we're taking care of currently. Unfortunately, we're constantly understaffed and rely a lot on volunteers. But you know how that goes. It's around-the-clock work. The honu don't care if it's a Sunday afternoon when they get tangled up in fishing line."

"It's the same in the Keys," replied Mark. "We've recently had to let some good people go and need to work with interns. Which, don't get me wrong, are great. But before Sienna took over eighteen months ago, the managers had run the place into the red. They had no idea how to fundraise and market and were just spending money with no funds coming in."

"I hate that part. It takes away so much time with the honu," said Josh. "So, Sienna's parents are the ones who started the place?"

"Yeah. She and her sister had a falling out. Sienna became a lawyer and moved to Boston. She never came back until her sister and brother-in-law died in a car crash."

"Wow, I'm so sorry to hear that."

"Yeah. Their three kids were instantly orphans."

Josh shook his head emphatically.

Mark swigged his drink. "So, another depressing subject: What happened between you and Melanie?"

Josh's brows furrowed. "I don't really like to talk about it. She cheated on me while I was on a trip to the French Frigate Shoals to do some research. Somehow, I turned into the bad guy because I was upset and couldn't forgive her. Now she's turning the kids against me and trying to cut my visitation rights."

"That's unbelievable, man. That's exactly how my marriage broke! Well, maybe not exactly. Isabel was always a bitch. But, come on, man, your kids will always love you. They're old enough and know you well enough to know you're a good guy."

"I think we need another round of drinks and some more upbeat subjects," Josh said as he waved at Stacey.

They could've talked for hours but after a while Josh noticed that Mark was getting quiet.

"You must be tired after that long flight. Let's call it a night."

Mark grinned. "Eleven years ago, I would have been able to party all night, but not anymore."

Chapter 3

*H*onu is the Hawaiian word for green sea turtles. Honu are the largest hard-shelled sea turtles in the world. They can live up to 60–80 years and weigh as much as 200–500 pounds.

They are unique among sea turtles since they are herbivores, eating mostly sea grasses and algae. Their diet is what gives their fat (not their shells) a greenish color, which is where they get their name from.

The honu is a symbol of a long life and mana (spiritual energy) in Hawaiian culture, their presence is said to bring good luck and peace. The honu is considered a form of 'aumakua or ancestral spirit for Hawaiians, offering lifelong protection and guidance. In Hawaii, it is considered bad karma to harm or disrespect an 'aumakua.

Honu have existed as a species for about 40–50 million years. The ancient Hawaiians harvested turtles, eating the meat, using the bones for fishhooks and keeping the shells for containers. Honu were also depicted in petroglyphs, showing their importance to the ancient Hawaiians. They were considered the property of the alii, the Hawaiian chiefs.

Mark put his laptop aside. He had terrible jet lag and had been up since 3 a.m. Since he couldn't sleep, he had started reading an article about the cultural and historical importance of honu in Hawaii.

His stomach was growling, so he finally went down to the kitchen to make coffee and find something to eat.

The dogs came running out of Josh's bedroom, wagging their tails and greeting him happily. Mark snuck up to Josh's door and closed it so Josh wouldn't wake up from the noise. He grinned at the loud snoring coming from the bed.

Unsure whether he should feed the dogs or not, he found some kibble and gave them half a cup each to calm them down a little. They wolfed the kibble down as if they were starving.

Just like the rest of the house, the kitchen was beautiful. Modern and functional with some remaining antique features. A large range surrounded by colorful antique tile took up one whole corner. Mark rounded the butcher block island and filled the coffee pot in the oversized sink.

Mark tried to quiet the dogs and not wake Josh up. The only thing he wanted was make some coffee, grab a banana and a cereal bar and get out of there. The coffee sputtered noisily. Once it was done, Mark let the dogs out and sat on the lanai. It was still pitch black, but a little light appeared on the eastern horizon.

The dogs enjoyed their unusual freedom this early in the morning. The scents were more intense, and they sniffed every inch of the overgrown back yard. Mark was nervous they'd bark, but after a while they returned to the lanai and settled down next to him. He sat at a teak table behind his laptop, enjoying his coffee, and called Sienna.

"Hi, Mark. Boy you're up early!"

"Yeah," he answered quietly so as not to wake anyone. "My

jet lag is bad."

"Well, I miss you already. How's everything going so far?"

"Awesome. I can't wait for you to see the house we're staying in. It's gorgeous. The property is full of tropical vegetation and fruit trees. The mangoes and papayas are the size of watermelons. Orchids are everywhere in the trees. Josh is only watching the house and staying here for two months."

"Is it okay with the owner for us to stay there too?"

"Yeah, Josh said he's cool with that. And it's not like you and I are going to destroy the house. We'll only be here to sleep."

"That's true," she replied. Her boss at the Boston law firm beeped in. "Mark, I'm sorry, I've got to go. Mr. C. is calling. I had to do some last-minute research for him yesterday."

"Okay, talk to you later, bye."

"Love you."

Mark sat there and realized how much he missed Sienna. They had never been separated this long. The thought he'd been having for a while popped back into his brain: there would never be a better opportunity to propose to Sienna than here on Maui. It would be really meaningful to buy her a locally-made ring. Maybe he'd get a chance to look for one before Sienna arrived.

Mark looked at his watch. It was almost 5:30. He felt like stretching his legs, so he looked for the dogs' leashes to take them for a walk. He grabbed them from where they hung by the front door. The dogs whined and jumped up on him, excited about the unusual attention as he attached their leashes to their collars.

The sun climbed higher in the sky, awakening the island. Roosters crowed in the distance. Tropical birds chirped noisily in the trees. Mark grinned. Some of the noises were similar to those in the Keys. Mark wondered how anyone could sleep past sunrise with this racket. A funny-looking flat, long animal that looked like a squirrel darted across the street. The dogs barked and dove for the animal. Mark shushed them as he skidded forward. He leaned all his weight back to stop them and keep from falling on his face.

"Quiet, guys!" They were quickly distracted by a different smell and walked at a fast pace, holding their noses down to the ground. It was quite a workout for Mark, but he enjoyed it. He tried to remember what the small squirrel-like animal was that lived in Hawaii. Oh, yeah, a mongoose. The pesky little animals were brought to Hawaii to fight rats that were damaging sugar cane in the 1800s. The idea backfired since rats were nocturnal and mongooses weren't. Plus, the mongooses ate lots of indigenous bird eggs such as the nene's, the official bird of the state of Hawaii.

Cars pulled out of the McMansion driveways as the neighbors headed to work. An attractive middle-aged woman in tennis attire driving a nice convertible slowed down and looked curiously at the handsome dark-haired man walking Clark Lang's dogs. Mark nodded at her, and she waved. She examined his muscular tanned legs in the rear-view mirror as she slowly drove down the road and made plans to stop by Clark's house later.

The sun was high in the sky. Mark looked at his watch again. It was almost 6 a.m., so he pulled the dogs around and

24

headed back to the house. Josh was up doing yoga on the lanai.

"Wow, that's impressive," said Mark as he stepped into the house. "I should join you!"

Josh grinned as he finished up with some deep breaths. Then he walked over to the kitchen. "Would you like a green smoothie?"

"I didn't know you were such a health nut. Yes, I'll have one."

"Sometimes I just try to make up for an evening like yesterday," replied Josh. "I had a health scare last year. My thyroid had to be removed and there was a chance of cancer, but I got lucky. Now I'm on thyroid meds and need to watch my weight."

"Wow, I had no idea. I'm glad it wasn't cancer."

"Thanks. Hey, and thanks for walking the dogs. How did they do?"

"Great, except when a mongoose ran across the street. I almost lost them when they tried to chase it."

"Oh no, I hope they didn't tear your arm out of its socket. They go nuts when they see wild animals."

"I was prepared, so it wasn't that bad. There was some lady in a nice sportscar checking me out," Mark said grinning.

Josh laughed. "Yes, there are some lonely housewives and widows here in the neighborhood. That might have been my neighbor Anne. She plays tennis around this time."

Mark laughed. "How far is it to the ocean? I'd really like to get in the habit of swimming in the morning. Especially with this damn jet lag."

"It's about a ten-minute bike ride or a four-minute drive.

You can borrow my bike, but we're going to get your rental car today. That way you have options to get around since we're not always going to be on the same schedule," said Josh as he started the blender full of green veggies, pineapple, lemon and ginger.

Mark nodded. He was going to ask Josh about getting a rental car, especially for the time when Sienna was there. The smoothie was ready. Josh handed Mark a glass.

"There are also eggs, milk and bread if you want to make yourself some breakfast. Please help yourself to anything you want. I'm gonna jump in the shower. Can you be ready to leave in thirty minutes?" He rinsed the pitcher and gulped down half of his own smoothie.

Mark opted for a couple pieces of toast and another coffee to keep the cleanup to a minimum. He had no idea Josh started work this early.

As if reading Mark's mind, Josh said, "Oh, and don't think I usually start working this early. We just got a call about a honu in distress. It's near Olowalu. Seems he's quite entangled in fishing line. The team is already on their way to get him, but you and I will meet them at the rescue."

"Okay, I'll be right back," said Mark as he rushed up the stairs to take a quick shower.

Thirty minutes later, the two men were driving up the road toward Ma'alaea.

They arrived at the Maui Turtle Rescue at the same time as the van with the entangled honu. Josh and Mark jumped out of the car and walked over to meet Josh's team.

"Hey, guys, this is my friend Mark from the Keys. Mark,

this is Kaipo, our vet tech, and this is our intern, Nora."

Kaipo, born and raised on Maui with Hawaiian ancestors, wiped the ocean salt on her Maui Turtle Rescue t-shirt before shaking Mark's hand and offering a noncommittal smile. Nora trailed her big blue eyes from head to toe over Mark with a flirtatious grin on her full lips before stretching her hand out to shake. Mark could tell by her attitude and her tiny designer shorts that she was trouble. She knew what power she had over men. He ignored it.

They went to the back of the van and opened the door to grab the container with the honu inside. It was so massive it took two people to lift it.

"Wow, he must be at least a hundred and fifty pounds," exclaimed Josh. He had already determined the honu was male due to his longer tail. Mark was on the other side of the honu, helping him. Kaipo walked ahead and opened a gate for them. Then she ran ahead again and opened a door to a little trailer-like building, the Turtle Rescue's treatment room. Nora had parked the van and was walking back to assist with the honu.

The honu had tight fishing line around his front flippers and his neck. It was almost strangling him. The rescue team heaved him onto a stainless-steel table. Josh assessed the damage quickly, grabbed a sharp knife and carefully started cutting the fishing line off.

The honu instinctively flinched, and Josh realized the fishing line had already embedded itself too deeply into the honu's skin.

He paused and took a closer look.

"I think we need to sedate this poor guy. He might be in

pain. This fishing line is cutting too deep into his skin and scales."

"Is there anything I can get?" asked Mark.

"Yes, over there in the drawer is a syringe and some alfaxalone. Let's give him about seventy-five milligrams. He's heavier than that, but I don't want to drug him too much."

Mark got the syringe and sedative out and prepared the medication. "You don't use propofol?"

"You can give him the alfaxalone via intramuscular injection. Propofol needs to be administered intravenously. We don't have time for that right now."

Mark nodded. Josh was right. He walked up to the honu and administered the medication into his pectoral muscle under his front legs.

Josh felt the honu relax and carefully cut the fishing line and pulled it out of the honu's skin. Nora cleaned the wounds. Once she was done, Josh applied plenty of betadine. The honu had suffered some other light cuts to his neck and deeper wounds to his front legs.

"Let's do some bloodwork and check his general condition. He looks quite healthy though. Let's hope that flipper recovers and doesn't have to be amputated," said Josh. Nora drew some blood, labeled the vial and got it ready to send out to a lab. The professionals worked their magic, and Mark could tell what a great team they were. They lifted the honu into a big plastic tub on wheels that Kaipo rolled into a little courtyard with several pools.

Josh explained, "He'll be able to rest and heal here."

Mark wiped the sweat from his forehead after they got the

honu settled.

"Well, that was a tense introduction to our rescue, but that's what our life here looks like," explained Josh. "Unfortunately, most of our cases are fishing line entanglements. Locals need to feed their families, and fishermen provide fish to local restaurants. We're trying to reduce the number of incidents by providing an easy method for anglers to discard their lines. We've installed bins and signs at countless fishing locations along Maui's shorelines and harbors.

"What's your procedure on keeping track of the honu? Do you microchip them?" Mark asked.

"We insert a PIT tag, Passive Integrative Transponder, under the skin of the turtles' hind flippers. They're about the size of a grain of rice and can be detected by a scanner. They're about the same as dogs' and cats' microchips. We also mototool tag them. We use a Dremel to safely etch the carapace with the initials of the island and the number of the stranding case that year. The groove is then filled with white paint. It's harmless for the honu but makes it easier for future observers to view the number without disturbing them."

"We only use the microchip, but that mototool tag is a great idea," replied Mark. "I might have to copy that in Florida if that's okay."

"Sure."

Josh had to answer some emails, so Kaipo gave Mark a tour of the Turtle Rescue. Just like in Turtle Key, there were various areas with different size basins. Unlike in the Keys, where there were a lot of permanent guests, the honu on Maui were mostly released again soon after treatment.

"We're quite overwhelmed currently," said Kaipo. "The turtle rescues on the Big Island and Oahu were closed recently, and we're getting all their honu too. We're the only turtle rescue in Hawaii right now."

They came up to a larger basin with several honu inside that all had tumors. Fibropapillomatosis, the debilitating disease that lots of sea turtles suffered from due to pollution. Treating these tumors was Mark's specialty.

"Here are your patients," said Kaipo.

Mark took a closer look at them. "Yup, that's FP. Poor guys. I hope we can help them soon."

Mark started feeling his jet lag and his 3 a.m. wake up. Kaipo had to assist one of the volunteers with a honu, and Mark turned around to head back to Josh's office. Josh was already walking toward him.

"Oh, there you are, I've been looking for you. I was able to carve out some time and thought we could go pick up your car in Kihei and have lunch somewhere."

"Sounds great. I'm having a jet lag moment right now, so eating some good old carbs might be the right thing to do. And some coffee would be great," he added, grinning.

"Maybe you should leave a bit early today and go and take a nap so you're not too tired tonight. I don't think it helps to go to bed at six. You've got to hang in there and try to stay awake until ten. Did Kaipo show you the honu with FP in the larger basin?"

"Yes, they really don't look as bad as ours in the Keys. I think pollution in Florida is much worse."

"We've had worse, but these will be good for you to

demonstrate on. Our other vet Billy is coming in tomorrow, so that'll be a good day. You should take it easy today."

Mark nodded.

They left the Maui Turtle Rescue and drove to a car rental in Kihei. Josh called them on the way and the car was ready when they arrived. "I thought we'd get you an SUV in case you ever have to transport a honu," said Josh.

They took care of the rental paperwork, and Mark followed Josh to a restaurant in Kihei, Pai'a Fish Market, where they ordered some delicious fish sandwiches. Mark felt much better after eating. The atmosphere around them bustled with tourists and beach goers. The ocean just across the street sparkled as the waves crashed ashore. They sat and watched the activities around them for a while. It was hot and sunny, but the trade winds were blowing, and it couldn't have been a more beautiful day.

"Okay, I've got to get back to work," said Josh. "Why don't you go home and get some rest. Actually, you can let the dogs out," he added. "And by the way, there's a Starbucks right up the road." He pointed a few buildings south.

That was exactly what Mark needed. Or, preferably, some locally grown Hawaiian coffee. He still remembered the aroma of his favorite Hawaiian coffee house in Upcountry from eleven years ago.

Since the meal and cool ocean breeze had given him a second wind, Mark stopped at the outdoor shopping mall, Shops at Wailea, on the way home. He milled around with the other tourists, popping in and out of different shops. Most were upscale designer stores and chains and, despite carrying tropical lines of clothing, lacked a local vibe. When he was about to call it a day, he spotted a small jewelry store. Mark walked over and looked in the window. Hawaiian heirloom plumeria engagement rings twinkled in the sunlight. A rainbow of gemstones glittered in the gold honu necklaces and other tropical designs. He saw the perfect gift for Sienna right away and knew she'd love something from a local place rather than a generic chain.

"Aloha," said Mark after stepping into the shop. "I love the engagement rings with the plumeria designs in your window."

"Aloha, I'm Julie. Nice to meet you. Let me show you a couple of options."

Mark was a quick shopper. He pointed at the first ring she showed him. "How much is this one?"

She named a rather high price which was to be expected in a place like this. He swallowed. Sienna was worth it.

"I'll take it."

"Which size do you need?"

A question he wasn't prepared for. He looked at Julie. She looked like she was about Sienna's size.

"What size are you?"

She smiled. She wasn't surprised. It happened quite often that her customers didn't know the correct ring size. "My ring size is seven."

"Okay, I'll take a size seven. I assume I can exchange it if it doesn't fit?"

"Yes, just bring your fiancée here, and we'll find the right size for her."

Mark had never spent several thousand dollars faster, but

he didn't blink once. He was a thousand percent sure about his intentions. He also picked out a silver bracelet with a honu pendant for his daughter Sydney.

After checking out, he drove straight home to make his own coffee and then go for a swim in the ocean. *I can't afford to go out for coffee anymore,* he thought, grinning as he glanced at the bag on the passenger seat. He parked, grabbed the bag and realized the neighbor from this morning was waiting for him at the front door.

Chapter 4

The neighbor held a box of malasadas in her hand. She walked up to him, her face beaming.

"Hi, I wanted to introduce myself and bring you something sweet. I'm Anne, Anne Marino. You must be new to the neighborhood. I live right next door." She handed him the box as she pointed at the mansion next door.

Mark was flabbergasted. He was too tired to deal with anyone right now.

"Thank you so much. I'm Mark Baldwin. I'm just visiting Josh for some work at the Maui Turtle Rescue. I don't know how well you know him. I'm only here for three weeks. Unfortunately, I only came home to change for an appointment."

"Oh," she said disappointed, examining Mark's chiseled jawbone, cupid bow lips and thick beard. She liked what she saw, and her marriage had ended quite a while ago. "Maybe we can have coffee another time. Or do you happen to play tennis?"

"Sure, but between work and plans with my girlfriend when she arrives in two days, it might get tight."

Anne's face visibly fell at the mention of Marks girlfriend.

"Well, I hope you have a great time on Maui." She pulled herself together instead of snapping at his rejection, walked back to her car and drove the fifty yards back to her house.

Mark waved. "And thanks for the malasadas!"

Mark watched the car leave, then walked into the house.

After letting the dogs out, he brewed himself a new pot of coffee and opened the box of malasadas, a Portuguese dessert comparable to donuts. They were brought to Hawaii by Portuguese laborers who came to work the plantations in the late 1800s. These were filled with lilikoi jam. Mark hadn't had a malasada in more than ten years. He felt bad for cutting off the neighbor like that, but he really needed some quiet time and had no desire to flirt with a lonely middle-aged lady. He grinned. *Maybe she'd be something for Josh...* But Josh probably wasn't ready for a new relationship after recently going through a tough divorce.

Mark stashed the bag with the ring and necklace in a safe place and was able to lie down and sleep despite the coffee. He set his alarm for 4 p.m. so he'd have enough time to go down to the beach before dinner and fell into a deep dreamless sleep.

At 4 p.m., Mark's alarm went off with his usual "by the seaside" ringtone. He felt groggy and could have probably slept until the next morning, but he forced himself to get up and not give in to his jet lag. It was 10 p.m. in Florida so he texted Sienna. *Are you getting excited about coming soon? It's really nice here.*

Yes, getting a little stressed, she replied. *Mr. C. is giving me all this research right before I leave because he knows I'll be gone for a week. But thank goodness there's not much to prepare, clothes are the same. She sent* a smile emoji.

Yes, he replied, *very casual here. Make sure to bring good sneakers or hiking shoes.*

Already packed. Sydney has been sleeping here, all going well.

That reminded Mark he needed to call Sydney. They had a brief conversation. Sydney was in heaven when she could spend time with Lilly and her big busy family. She was rather lonely at her mom's house.

Josh texted Mark. *I forgot that tonight is my night with the kids. Will be going straight to dinner with them. Could you let the dogs out and feed them?*

Sure. Have fun. Mark decided to go into Lahaina for dinner. It would be a bit of a drive, but he enjoyed walking around there.

Before dinner, he put on his bathing suit, slathered himself with some reef-safe sunscreen and drove down to the beach. He was amazed about how well he remembered everything after eleven years. The beach at the Fairmont was the closest one, and there were free parking spaces in the road next to the big hotel. He walked down to the ocean and took in the beautiful atmosphere.

It was so different than the Keys. While the water in the Keys was turquoise like the Caribbean, it was calm and could be rather murky in the summertime since it was so shallow. The water here was wild and rough. Mark looked back at the beautiful hotel property and the oceanfront villas he'd probably never be able to afford. After putting his towel and car key on a rock, he made his way through the cold, refreshing waves. He dove under the approaching wave and came out on the other side of the break. Then he quickly donned his swim goggles and began swimming along the shoreline with quick rhythmic freestyle strokes. He switched to backstroke and enjoyed the roaring salty water. He had started swimming as a method of stress relief since his divorce and had remained an avid swimmer since then.

Mark dove down to see if he'd discover anything interesting. A honu swam in the distance, yellow tang fish darted between some lava rock. He came back up, turned around and swam back to the other side of the beach. After the waves pushed him ashore, he wrapped his towel around his shoulders and sat down on a rock. Watching families and kids playing in the sand, he felt homesick and wished Sienna and the kids were here with him. At least Sienna was arriving in two days. He looked at his watch. It was too late to call her.

Mark had let some old friends know he was in town, so he went back to the house to change and made his way over to Lahaina to meet them at Betty's Beach Café.

As he drove down Honoapiilani Highway between the West Maui Mountains on the right side and the ocean on the left, he suddenly realized where he was. Mark had almost passed the fruit stand where his old girlfriend Palila and her mother used to work. *We could really use some fruit and fresh vegetables for the house,* he thought. The gravel crunched as he took a sharp right into the driveway and parked his car beneath the shade of a palm tree. He rolled the windows down and sat watching the locals selling their produce. As Mark listened to the birds trilling around him, long suppressed memories came flooding back.

FLASHBACK

approx. 11 years ago @ Olowalu Beach

Palila and Mark camped at Camp Olowalu. It was dark. They'd just come out of the water and were alone on the beach. Palila took her bikini top off and hung it on a branch to dry. She didn't bother covering herself with a towel. She called Mark who was right behind her, walked up to him and started kissing him wildly. They fell into the sand.

BACK TO PRESENT TIME

Palila, his first big love. He had met the tall strong-willed Hawaiian woman surfing at Ho'okipa Beach. Her long black hair, gorgeous dark eyes and goddess-like body had caught his and many others' attention.

She was well-known among the surfers as a daredevil. Her feet were practically glued to the surfboard, and she never wiped out. She flew with ease over the highest waves. Talent scouts pursued her, offering her a glamorous life as a prosurfer, but that meant she'd have to go train in Oahu or California, then constantly travel. Palila secretly imagined traveling around the world as a pro-surfer but just laughed at them. She was never going to leave her beloved Maui. She was a hard worker, and her widowed mother needed help on her farm and at the produce market. There were too many strings attached: Her mother would never let her go, and she'd never abandon her ohana, even though she worked like a slave.

One day she saw Mark trying to surf at Ho'okipa Beach. A tall man, just out of college, with the thickest dark hair, bright blue eyes, the sweetest smile and a chiseled chin. He might have been surfing for the first time, and he was really struggling. The waves were too rough for a beginner, but he was determined and kept going out again and again. Palila gave him some pointers.

"If you want to practice at an easier beach, I'll be glad to help you out," she proposed. They met outside of Lahaina the next day where the waves were nothing compared to the enormous swells at Ho'okipa Beach.

Palila, who was two years older than Mark, didn't only teach him how to surf. She also taught the inexperienced young man passion and love. She worked as a hula dancer at one of the biggest luaus on the island and taught Mark about Hawaii's history and culture. Palila was a free spirit, and they made love everywhere: under the stars on the beach, in the forest while camping, in the ocean. Everything Palila did was full of passion, and she loved Mark with all her body and soul. For a few months, they were inseparable. Mark lived at plantation in Wailuku with Palila and her mother, and in his spare time he helped wherever he could. Everybody thought they'd get married one day. Mark had loved her and their life together. Palila, named after the palila bird, a critically endangered species of honeycreeper, had also been as free as a bird.

Once it became clear that Josh was going to get the only veterinarian position at the Maui Turtle Rescue, Mark had no choice but to look elsewhere for work. The Florida Keys were the next best option. And his uncle's veterinary clinic was in Orlando. Palila was upset that he was even considering leaving and started hating him with the same passion she had loved him. She'd expected him to stay and toss his career aside. Palila disappeared from the Wailuku area. Her mother refused to speak to Mark and let him know that he wasn't welcome at the plantation anymore. Mark eventually left, broken-hearted, without seeing or speaking with Palila again. When he tried contacting her from the Keys, she was too proud to reply.

Mark swallowed as he sat in his car looking at the produce stand. When Josh had asked him to come to Maui, he had thought about Palila briefly. But he had moved on a long time ago, and he was happy now.

Mark wondered whether Palila and her mother were still here and whether they'd all recognize each other. Only a few teenagers worked the stand right now. He got out of his car and walked up, choosing a few avocadoes, a pineapple, two mangoes and some lilikoi. He asked the young man at the cash register, "Do you know Palila Mahoe and her mom?"

"The mom died a long time ago, but Palila still owns the stand," replied the man, pointing at a sign that said, *Palila's Produce*. "She lives in the trailer over there, but she's not here right now."

Mark was shocked. Palila lived in a trailer? Was she homeless? Her family had been well-off ten years ago. They had owned a thriving plantation in the Wailuku area. Mark thought about leaving a message, but then an older car drove up. A middle-aged woman got out of the passenger side. She certainly looked like Palila. A little girl climbed out of the back seat. Her skin was much lighter than Palila's, making her look like a hapa - part Hawaiian and part Caucasian.

"Mahalo for the ride," said the woman. She slammed the door shut and waved goodbye as the car departed. She turned around and walked toward the stand. When she saw Mark, she froze and grabbed the girl's hand. It was indeed Palila, and she wasn't happy to see Mark.

Chapter 5

Palila, is that you?" Mark asked carefully. The woman didn't reply and pulled the girl behind her toward the trailer. The girl turned around and looked curiously at Mark with bright blue eyes. Just like his own.

"Palila!"

The woman turned around and glared at him. The awkward silence grew between them as they stood there, staring at each other.

"Palila, don't you recognize me? Can we talk?"

They were both eleven years older, but either she hadn't aged well, or she just didn't look good right now. She had lost a lot of weight, her skin was pale, and she had a scarf wrapped around her head. So much of this formerly vibrant woman had vanished. She limped toward the trailer, without answering, obviously embarrassed that Mark was seeing her in her current state, but then she stopped and turned around one more time.

"What's there to talk about?" she replied, her eyes filling with tears. She pulled the reluctant girl along who was curious about the stranger. Mark followed them to the camper. Suddenly, Palila stumbled, collapsed and passed out.

The girl kneeled next to her. "Makuahine, Mama!" Mark

froze, then also kneeled, trying to figure out what had happened to Palila. "Please help my mom. She is really sick!"

Mark held his fingers against her neck, checking for a pulse. Then he called 911.

"Hi, a woman collapsed here at Palila's Produce stand on Honoapiilani Highway, across from Olowalu Beach. Do you know where I mean, a few miles before the Pali Tunnel? I'm not sure what's wrong. She has a pulse but she's not responding."

A few minutes later, the ambulance arrived with flashing lights. Palila had woken up and tried to refuse the paramedics' treatment, but she couldn't get up.

"I have no health insurance," she said weakly, trying to lift her head.

"We're going to take you with us and treat you anyway, ma'am. You know the protocol," said the paramedic in a friendly manner. They checked her vitals and lifted her onto a stretcher. As they carried her to the ambulance, he said to Mark, "We're taking her to Maui Memorial Medical Center. The daughter can't ride with us. She usually gets picked up by a friend."

Mark was puzzled that this seemed to be a regular occurrence. He nodded, looking at the girl. "I'll follow you with her this time."

The girl cried as her mother was pushed into the ambulance.

Mark knew exactly what to do. He kneeled next to the little girl and said, "I promise, everything will be okay with your mom. What's your name?"

"Nalu," she said shyly. She looked up at him with tears in

her eyes and a trembling lip.

Seeing the little girl up close, Mark was practically looking into a mirror. He blinked a few times as he processed what this meant, then pushed his feelings aside rather than let them distract him.

"Your mom might need some things in the hospital like pajamas, some new underwear, a toothbrush and toothpaste. Can you pack a little duffel bag for her? Do you have a key to the trailer?"

"Yeah," she whispered. "I have to be here by myself a lot when my mom's working."

"Okay, please pack a little bag for her just in case she needs to stay there. We'll follow her to the hospital."

Nalu opened the trailer door and disappeared inside. After a few minutes, she came back out carrying a recyclable shopping bag with some of her mom's belongings.

When Mark and Nalu arrived at the hospital, Palila had already been admitted and was in an exam room, waiting for test results. A nurse was putting in an IV line. An older Hawaiian doctor stepped into the room. "Mrs. Mahoe, can I speak in front of your visitors, or would you rather speak in private?"

She capitulated, realizing she had nobody to take care of Nalu in case something happened.

"I have no secrets. Go ahead."

The doctor held out a hand to Mark. "Hi, I'm Dr. Kahale, the leading oncologist at this hospital." He flipped through Palila's chart. "Well, Mrs. Mahoe, as I told you last time, there's nothing we can do anymore."

"What do you mean there's nothing you can do?" Mark asked. "She collapsed!"

"She has stage four ovarian cancer that's already metastasized and spread to her liver and bones."

Mark reeled back at the news.

"I'll give you some more samples of the pain medication to take home, and here's a prescription in case you're able to fill it," he said, glancing at Mark.

Dr. Kahale said goodbye to Palila and Nalu and quietly asked Mark, "Could I speak to you outside for a moment?"

Mark followed him into the hallway, still shocked about Palila's grim diagnosis.

Dr. Kahale closed Palila's door. "Are you Nalu's father?" Mark didn't quite know what to say. It was a lot to process.

He replied honestly, "I actually didn't know until today, but I guess I might be her father."

"As you may have previously known or just found out, Mrs. Mahoe is dying. She has a couple of weeks at the most. At first, she declined any further treatment, and now it's too late to do anything. The cancer has spread too far. The problem is that she's still working herself to death and not taking care of herself. Is there anything you can do to help? She really needs a roof over her head, running water and regular meals. Not the trailer she's in right now. It's moldy and making her condition even worse. And it's not healthy for her daughter either. I can keep her here for two nights without getting in trouble with my boss. But after that she needs a better place to stay. And Nalu too. She can't stay in the trailer by herself."

"I'm staying at a friend's house, but of course I'll take care of Nalu for now. And I'll try to find a place for Palila to stay."

The doctor put his hand on Mark's shoulder, said, "Mahalo. You're a good man," and walked away.

Mark's ears started ringing and he leaned heavily against the wall. What had he gotten himself into? Did Palila even want his help? How would he find a place for her to stay? And how would he care for Nalu who obviously had to go to school while he had to work. First, he called his friends in Lahaina and let them know he couldn't make it for dinner. Then he stepped back into Palila's room where she and Nalu were waiting for him.

Palila sat up and cleared her throat. "Well, I might as well tell you both. Nalu, this is your dad, and Mark, Nalu is your daughter." Then she fell back into her pillows.

Nalu bowed her head, looking up at Mark with just her eyes, waiting for his reaction. She looked scared. Scared he'd reject her. And scared about her mom's and her own future.

Mark had questions he wanted to discuss with Palila without Nalu around. What was Palila going to do with Nalu if he hadn't coincidentally shown up? She didn't seem to have any other relatives or people she could rely on. He was shocked about the entire situation.

He tried to respond in a way that wouldn't hurt Nalu. "I can kind of see that. She sure looks like me, doesn't she?" He smiled at Nalu with her bright blue eyes, and she looked back at him. Even though her mother was dying, and her world was upside down, she knew this man was going to help her. She wouldn't be all alone. But she had seen too many boyfriends pass through over the years, including abusive ones, so she remained careful and distant. She hadn't learned trust.

Far too early on for a child, Nalu acted like a grown up. She helped her overwhelmed mom, who was working herself to the bones, with chores on the plantation. But even that had been better than the embarrassment of living in the trailer with no running water after losing the plantation.

Often, she had gone to school in dirty clothes because they hadn't made it to the laundromat in Wailuku. She got bullied and ridiculed.

No one had been able to drive her after her mother got too sick. She couldn't take the school bus anymore because the trailer wasn't on its route. Eventually, Palila started homeschooling Nalu. She excelled and went quickly from a fourth to a fifth grade level, but she was lonely and unhappy.

Her mom still owned and ran the fruit stand. Without their plantation, she had to buy the produce and resell it for a profit, which was too low to pay the workers and stand fees.

"Can you take Nalu for two days until I'm released from the hospital?" asked Palila. "I have a friend who has been taking her when I'm in the hospital, but she's going out of town. Sometimes I've had to leave her alone."

Mark nodded and clenched his fists. That trailer on the main road was certainly not a place for a ten-year-old to be all by herself. Palila continued weakly. "I'm scheduled to go stay in Hāna with a friend in two days, so I'll take her back then."

Mark turned toward Nalu. "Don't you go to school?"

"I'm homeschooled," she replied.

"Okay, so we'll drive back to the camper and get some of your things. Then we'll go and get something to eat. I'm starving, how about you?"

Nalu nodded.

"Do you like pizza? I know a very good pizza place in Kihei."

She nodded again.

Mark's behavior encouraged Palila. He was obviously used to children. After so many years of being stubborn and independent, she had to let go. She knew Mark was a kind-hearted man, and her daughter was safe. She fell into a deep sleep. The strong medication dripping through the IV was finally doing its job.

Mark stretched out his hand to take Nalu's. She hesitated but got up from her mother's bed and put her hand in his. Together they walked down the hallway to let the nurse know they were leaving.

Chapter 6

Mark and Nalu drove back to the trailer where Nalu packed a few clothes and her laptop for school. The produce stand was closed, and the employees were gone for the day. Mark noticed a drying rack full of clothes behind the camper.

"Shall we take those clothes inside in case it rains?" he asked Nalu.

"Oh, yeah." She hurried to gather the clothes off the rack. Mark folded the rack and stood it up against the back of the trailer.

"How long have you been living here?" he asked.

"About three months," Nalu replied.

"That can't be easy. Did you still live at the plantation before that?"

"Yeah, but Mom couldn't afford it anymore."

Mark was surprised. The plantation had been in Palila's family for generations and must've been paid off. But of course, there were always other expenses such as property taxes and utility bills.

"What about your Tutu? Has she been dead for a long time?"

"Yeah, I can't even remember her. I think she died when I was a baby."

Mark wondered what had happened. Palila's mother had been a strong healthy woman.

They stopped at Mark's favorite old pizza joint in Kihei. With the pizza carton and two waters in hand, they sat on the rock wall to eat. They were right on the beach. The bright red sun was disappearing into the ocean, painting the sky like an impressionist seascape. They discovered a honu lying at the shoreline just a hundred yards away. Mark told Nalu about his work with sea turtles. She was very interested and told him she loved honu. She showed him the honu necklace she wore.

There was a little moment of silence when Mark told Nalu he was here for only four weeks and would then return to the Turtle Sanctuary in Florida where he usually worked. Neither of them wanted to think about what would happen to Nalu when Palila was gone and Mark left too.

"So, I'm just staying with a friend who's housesitting for another friend. But there's a second guest room which I think you can use. We'll ask him when he gets home."

"I hope it's okay," Nalu replied quietly. "I don't want to be a nuisance."

Mark looked at her. She was too mature for her age. He felt bad that she was having such a tough childhood, and he wished he could help her and her mother. Then Sienna crossed his mind. How was he going to tell her about this? She'd be on her way to Maui in less than forty-eight hours, and he suddenly had a new family to take care of! He stopped those thoughts and concentrated on Nalu who was right here with him.

"Do you like dogs?"

Nalu's eyes flew wide open at his question. "Of course! We used to have one, but he was old and died."

Mark remembered that Palila's family had owned a beautiful Australian shepherd. "Was that Pele?"

Nalu smiled at the dog's name and nodded.

"Well, wait until you see the two golden retrievers that my friend's watching. They're nuts. You'll be a big help if you can play with them and tucker them out."

Her face beamed with anticipation. He had certainly found her soft spots mentioning dogs and honu.

When they were done with dinner, they drove the last few miles to the house in Wailea.

On the way there, Mark drove into a shopping plaza and parked in front of a groovy 70s-looking VW bug belonging to a shave ice stand. The sign said "Peace Love Shave Ice" in rainbow letters.

"Let's have some shave ice," he said.

Nalu was beside herself with happiness. She hadn't had shave ice in a long time. Her sweet little face beamed as they stepped up to the stand. A friendly middle-aged woman with her hair bunched up on top of her head greeted them.

"Aloha, guys! What can I get for you?"

"Hey, Allison, is that you?" asked Mark, "The last time I was here was eleven years ago."

"Yes, it is me!" She examined his face, trying to recognize him. Mark and Josh had hung out here constantly. "You're Josh's friend, aren't you? Wow, that's really a long time ago! I'm glad you caught me. I'm moving to Kauai, and a friend is taking over this location."

"Wow, lucky to see you one more time. We'll have to come and visit you in Kauai. Are you going to have a stand there too?"

"Yep. I just got married, but still got to work. The bills don't pay themselves."

"Congrats."

"And this is your daughter?"

"Yes, this is Nalu."

"Hi, Nalu, what's your favorite kind of shave ice? How about lilikoi?"

Nalu looked pleased that Mark had introduced her as his daughter. "Yes, how did you know?"

"You look like a lilikoi kind of girl." Allison smiled and turned on the ice machine. She let the ice "snow" down into a cup which she compacted and shaped into a ball. Then she poured syrup onto the shave ice and handed it to Nalu with a spoon.

"How about you, Mark?"

He looked at the list of flavors and hesitated. "I think I'll have pineapple-orange, please."

"Didn't you always have that?"

"I think I did!"

She made his ice and handed it to him. A few other customers came up. Allison had to take care of them, so Mark and Nalu sat down and enjoyed their treat.

It was dark by the time they finished, and Nalu yawned.

"We should get you settled," said Mark. They said goodbye to Allison and wished her good luck in Kauai, then finally drove to the house. Nalu was tired, but she got another burst of energy when she saw the two golden retrievers. For a little while, she forgot about all her problems. She took the dogs out in the backyard and played with them for an entire hour. While she was outside, Josh came home. Mark spoke with him about Palila and his "new" daughter. Josh was almost as shocked as Mark himself and had to sit down.

"I need a beer," he said. "I'm so sorry about Palila. Of course, Nalu can stay here for two days, but what are we going to do for a long-term solution for Palila? She can't stay when Sienna gets here. I think that might be a little much for Sienna."

"I have to talk to Palila without Nalu around," replied Mark. "The whole situation was awkward at the hospital when Palila told both of us that I'm her dad. I'd really like to know what solution she had for Nalu, since she didn't know I was coming. But as far as Palila's concerned, it seems she has something lined up in Hāna. She's going there in two days once she gets discharged from the hospital."

"Thank goodness," said Josh. "So, they'll both be gone by the time Sienna gets here."

Mark opened a beer for himself, his eye twitching nervously. "Yeah. It's going to be interesting to tell her this whole story. Do you know what I was going to do? I was going to propose to her! And now I suddenly have another daughter."

Nalu stepped inside the house and heard Mark's last few words.

She paled and ran back out to the yard where she put her arms around Arnold Palmer and started crying.

Mark looked at Josh who looked back at him and shrugged.

Mark set his beer down and followed Nalu outside. He put his hand on her back. "Nalu, I didn't mean what I just said in a negative way. I'm very happy that I found you. But you know, it's quite a shock for me too. I didn't know I had a daughter for ten years. I promise, we'll figure everything out."

"Will I have to come and live with you in Florida?"

"Maybe. We'll talk to your mom about it."

"But I wanna stay in Maui." She sobbed even more.

"Let's wait and see what your mom says. And, hey, maybe you'd like Florida. You know, I have another daughter named Sydney. She's seven. You guys might get along well."

Nalu stopped crying and looked at him with shining eyes.

"So, I have a sister? Maybe you guys can all move to Maui," she replied. Her face lit up again.

"Nothing's etched in stone," he said. "Come inside and I'll introduce you to my friend Josh. He works at the Maui Turtle Rescue and rescues honu. You'll really like him. I'm sure he'll show you the place and the recovering honu if you ask him nicely."

Mark took Nalu's hand, and she followed him inside. Josh's eyes darted back and forth between them. "There's no doubt that you're her dad." Then he said to Nalu, "Hey there, Nalu, it's nice to meet you. I'm Josh. I used to know your mom before you were born."

Nalu nodded. She had already decided she liked Josh with his cool long hair. And for letting her stay here.

"So, let's get you settled, Nalu. Josh, can Nalu stay in the second guest room across from mine?"

"Yes, the bed has clean sheets, and everything is ready.

Nalu, is there anything you like to eat that we can get you tonight or tomorrow?"

She thought for a moment but didn't want to make extra work for them. "I like everything," she said. "I usually eat a banana and some toast with peanut butter and jelly for breakfast. And drink milk."

"I think we have that in the house. Please let us know if you think of anything else. When do you go to school in the morning?" Josh asked then looked at Mark. "I assume we have to drive her?"

"No, I homeschool," she said.

"So, you'll be here all day." Josh smiled. "Arnold Palmer and Ben Hogan will be very happy about the company."

"Why do they have such funny names?" asked Nalu.

"Arnold Palmer and Ben Hogan were famous golfers. My friend, the guy who owns the house, is a professional golfer too."

Nalu nodded.

"Why don't I show you your room, Nalu," said Mark. "Do you have any homework you have to do?"

"Yeah." She sighed and followed him upstairs, but she was quite pleased when she saw her beautiful room for the next two days.

Chapter 7

The next morning, Mark's jet lag woke him at 4 a.m. *A bit better than yesterday,* he thought. He called Sienna but couldn't enjoy the conversation because the Palila and Nalu matter loomed over him. This was something he wanted to tell her in person, not on the phone. Sienna felt something was wrong and asked, but he lied and said that everything was okay. He had just told Sienna his first lie in their relationship and didn't feel good about it.

After they ended the call, Mark heard noises from the room next door and walked into the hallway to hear better. Nalu was either having a bad dream or sobbing. He carefully opened the door and stepped into the guestroom. Nalu was under her covers in the queen poster bed, curled in the fetal position and crying into her pillow. She didn't hear him enter. He sat down on the side of her bed and put his arm around her back. "Shhhh, shhhh. Nalu. I know you're worried about your mom," he whispered.

She startled, realizing Mark was there. Then she continued sobbing. "I've never been away from her."

"Tomorrow, she'll be released from the hospital. It's only one more night."

"But then she'll die." Nalu sobbed harder.

There was nothing comforting Mark could say to that. He just rubbed her back and said, "I'm so sorry."

He sat there comforting her until she fell back asleep. Her sobs quieted in her sleep until her calm breathing indicated that Mark could leave. He felt drained and saddened. As he stepped out of the room, he wondered if it was a good idea to leave her alone at the house all day, but he really had no other choice. Today, he was to demonstrate his laser technique to Josh and another vet who volunteered at the Maui Turtle Rescue.

Mark read a little, then he couldn't lie in bed any longer and got up to go for a quick swim at the Fairmont. He checked briefly on Nalu, but her breath sounded deep and relaxed.

The sun was just going up for another beautiful day on Maui as he parked his car and walked down to the water. The beach was empty except for a honu hanging out by some lava rocks and few myna birds darting through the sky. Mark stepped into the water, dove headfirst into the waves and came up on the other side, thinking about Palila and Nalu non-stop and how Sienna's reaction was going to be when she heard the news. With powerful strokes and strong kicks, he swam along the shoreline, slowly relaxing. Every second stroke, he'd come up for a quick breath. After swimming hard for twenty minutes, he finally slowed down and turned onto his back, just treading water for a few minutes. He finally walked back to the beach and sat on the rocks, listening to the meditative sounds of the ocean, until some employees showed up and started setting up lounge chairs. That meant it was time to head back.

Later in the morning, at a more human time, Mark and Josh left in two different cars to the Maui Turtle Rescue. Mark told Nalu that he'd pick her up for lunch and they'd go visit her mother in the hospital. That wouldn't give her too much alone time to feel sad. He realized though that he didn't have to worry about her with Arnold Palmer and Ben Hogan around. As long as she had those two happy pups to take care of, she was going to be fine.

As often happened at the Maui Turtle Rescue, things didn't go according to plan. An emergency got in the way. A honu had been attacked by a shark and severely injured on the Big Island this morning. Volunteers rescued her, and she was on her way to Kahului by plane. At least one additional person had to go pick her up with Kaipo. The honu was injured so badly that Kaipo needed someone to assist her and ride with the honu in the back of the van. Since Josh was too busy, Mark volunteered to accompany Kaipo, and his demonstration was postponed again.

"How are you acclimating to Maui?" asked Kaipo.

"Well, it's not hard to get used to staying in that nice mansion in Wailea with Josh. My house isn't half as nice. The Keys are almost as expensive as Maui. I live in a little old cottage with my girlfriend and four kids," he said grinning.

They both laughed. The house wasn't typical for Josh, a minimalist who couldn't care less about status symbols.

As they arrived at the intersection where the road split toward the Olowalu produce stand, Mark started worrying about Nalu again. He knew she was probably busy with school, or should be, but he gave her a quick call to check in.

She answered her phone and told him she was in the middle of a Zoom call with her teacher.

"Sorry to interrupt you while you're studying," said Mark. He hung up and stared out the window.

Kaipo could tell something was wrong. "Is everything okay?" she asked.

He hesitated to tell her about this delicate private matter, but people at the Maui Turtle Rescue were so tight, she would probably hear about it anyway.

"Yesterday, I found out I have a daughter," he said matter-of-factly.

"*What?*" She almost swerved as she took her eyes off the road a bit too long to look at him.

"Yup. I had no idea about her. I was involved with a woman eleven years ago. She got pregnant back then and never told me. She broke off all contact with me because she was upset that I got a job in the Keys and had to leave. I had no other choice! There was only one job for one veterinarian at the Turtle Rescue, and Josh got it."

"Wow, and now you're already taking care of the daughter's school and everything?"

"It gets worse. The mother has terminal cancer and is dying."

"I'm so sorry to hear that. That's very sad," she replied.

"Yeah, and I'm not sure how I'm going to tell my girlfriend Sienna. She's arriving tomorrow."

"Well, it's not like you knew," Kaipo replied. "But I know

what you mean. She's gonna be upset no matter what."

Mark nodded. He knew she was right.

They parked the van at Kahului airport and walked up to the Mokulele Airlines counter since this was live inter-island freight. The airport employees all knew Kaipo and greeted her with high fives and shakas. One of them drove up in a cart with a lift-gate, on it a giant crate containing the honu. Mark and Kaipo walked ahead of him toward the van. All three of them pushed the crate into the van. Mark looked briefly at the honu whose carapace seemed quite damaged from the shark bite. He guessed her weight and gave her a shot of ketamine to relieve the pain. Then they headed back to Ma'alaea Harbor, Mark sitting in the back, keeping an eye on the honu.

Josh was waiting as they pulled up to the side of the building. He opened the van's back door and looked inside. "How's she doing?" he asked.

"Her injury is significant," replied Mark. "I gave her some ketamine for pain."

Kaipo, in her stoic manner, walked away quietly and returned, pushing a dolly. They lifted the container down onto the dolly and pushed it over to the treatment room to examine the honu. They treated her injured carapace and put her into a bigger open tub in the shade next to some others where she could rest and heal.

Josh said, "Once again, there's not much we can do besides let her rest. One of the fantastic things about a honu's carapace is that it can slowly repair itself and grow back. We can also help with laser treatment."

Mark looked at his watch. It was time to pick up Nalu and

take her to visit her mom. He let Josh know he was leaving for a while and jumped into his SUV. Nalu was already waiting, and twenty minutes later they arrived at the hospital.

Palila was sitting up in her bed, ready for their visit. With medication pumping through her, she was in better spirits. A nurse was leaving the room, and they laughed about something funny one of them had said in Hawaiian. Palila still looked thin and weak, but she seemed more upbeat than yesterday.

"Aloha, Makuahine," said Nalu. She rushed over to her bed, giving Palila a great big hug, tears streaming from her eyes.

Palila hugged her daughter back, closing her eyes and taking it all in.

Mark remained in the background to give mother and daughter some time, but Palila waved him in closer.

"I'm sorry about yesterday. I hadn't eaten all day, and I still have that blood sugar issue."

"No worries," replied Mark. He realized he wouldn't be able to talk to Palila in private, so he had no chance to ask about her plans for Nalu's future. Palila and Nalu cuddled and caressed each other's head, hair and cheeks. Mark saw the love between them and felt endlessly sad for mother and daughter.

He wanted to give them some privacy and asked, "Is there anything I can get you guys from the cafeteria? I could use a snack."

Nalu turned around with a big toothy smile. "Yeah, I'm starving. Could I get a sandwich?"

"Sure, and how about you, Palila?"

She pointed at her lunch tray. "I'm fine. Mahalo. The food

here's pretty good."

Mark went down to the cafeteria. When he came back up, he and Nalu ate their sandwiches quietly. Palila watched them, amazed about their similarities. They even moved their heads and chewed the same. Even though she dreaded it, Palila knew she and Mark had to talk in private.

As soon as he and Nalu were done eating, she fished some dollar bills out of her purse and asked, "Nalu, you know those little lilikoi pies they have in the cafeteria? Can you go down and get us a couple?"

Nalu loved being independent and running errands by herself. She grabbed the dollar bills and ran out the door.

Mark looked at her sternly. "Why didn't you tell me about her?"

"Would that have changed anything?"

"I don't know, but I could have supported you. I owe you child support for ten years."

"No, you don't. She's my daughter, and I decided to have her on my own."

Mark didn't want to argue. He knew how sick she was.

"So, what was your plan for Nalu before I suddenly showed up here?"

"We're going to Hāna tomorrow to stay with my friend Lani and her family. She is a hapa, just like Nalu. She and her husband Max offered to take Nalu. They are the kindest people I know, and her family is awesome. There is also a healer in Hāna I've known for a while who will accompany me during the last days with herbs, teas, massages and meditation. She knows what she's doing."

"Hāna is far away from a hospital if there's an emergency."

"There won't be any emergencies. I'll die and that's it. Ana, the healer, isn't doing this for the first time."

Mark's mouth fell open. What Palila needed, in his opinion, was a hospice and medical assistance, not some healer two hours away from the closest hospital. He kept his opinion to himself though. It was none of his business.

"Would you mind if I came and met this family you want Nalu to live with? Now that I'm here, might you change your mind and let her live with me?"

She wasn't sure what to say or do now that Mark had suddenly shown up. Maybe Nalu did belong with her biological father. Palila had grown up without a father herself. But she also couldn't stand the thought of Nalu having to leave Maui, the home of her ancestors.

"Sure, come and visit us."

"I'll have to talk to my girlfriend. She's arriving tomorrow."

Palila froze. She forced herself to nod so Mark wouldn't see her shock. A girlfriend. What did she expect? But, in her condition, nothing mattered anymore. She was just trying to make peace with having to leave Nalu so soon. Nothing else mattered.

Chapter 8

Palila asked Mark to help her drive to Hāna. It was a strenuous drive, and she didn't have the energy anymore. After his laser presentation the next morning, he took the afternoon off. He left the Maui Turtle Rescue and went straight to the trailer on Honoapi'ilani Highway to meet Palila and Nalu.

They waited for Mark in front of the locked-up camper with all their belongings packed in a few duffel bags and larger shopping bags. It was midafternoon, so Mark would probably be driving back in the dark, but he had driven the dangerous road so many times, it didn't bother him.

Palila had wrapped a scarf around her head. She was still beautiful despite her weight loss, though her sad eyes had lost their sparkle. Mark's throat knotted as he remembered the vibrant woman he had loved eleven years ago. He looked forward and concentrated on the road.

They drove in and out of Pai'a, the surfing town, bustling with tourists walking up and down streets full of shops, cafes and galleries.

Mark asked, "Would you mind if I stop at Ho'okipa Beach and take a look at the honu? Josh mentioned that one of the 'regulars' in Ma'alaea Harbor hasn't been seen in a while, a younger honu with a tattoo on its shell from a previous stay at the Maui Turtle Rescue. Mostly, they like to hang out in the same places, but this one has been missing, so we're checking all the other beaches."

Nalu's face lit up. "Oh, yeah, let's go and see the honu!"

Palila nodded. "We're not on a schedule, take your time and stop whenever you want. We'd like to stop at Ke'anae Peninsula if that's okay. Auntie Charlene bought some banana bread for us to share with Lani."

"Of course. I love banana bread. Don't they always close earlier in the day?" Mark asked.

"Yeah, but Charlene already organized some for us. We don't have to stop at the stand."

They arrived at the parking lot leading down to Ho'okipa Beach. Mark and Nalu jumped out of the SUV while Palila waited in the car. She rolled down the window and looked out at the ocean, lost in her thoughts, her scarf blowing in the wind. This was where she and Mark had met surfing eleven years ago.

More than twenty beautiful massive honu were basking in the sun on the east side of the beach, closest to the cliffs right by the parking lot. Some were already dry from sitting a while, some were still wet from the ocean, their carapaces glistening in the sun. Several tourists stood at a respectful distance, admiring them. One of them, looking through his camera lens, walked closer and closer until he was about four feet away from the honu.

Mark shouted, "Sir, these sea turtles are protected. You're supposed to stay at least ten feet away from them."

Other tourists chimed in, agreeing with Mark.

The man looked up, startled. "Who are you, telling me what to do?" He turned back and continued taking pictures, almost stepping on another honu.

"I work with the Maui Turtle Rescue and kindly ask you to keep a safe distance. You're harassing the honu right now, and they're protected by federal and state law."

"You're bothering them much more by yelling at me like that," said the man. He backed off, red-faced and cursing as he walked away.

Mark, Nalu and the other tourists shook their heads as they watched him leave. There were always a few obnoxious people who didn't care about the rules.

Mark took out a pair of binoculars and examined the honus' shells from a safe distance. He spotted two that had the Maui Turtle Rescue's mototool tag etched into their carapaces but not the juvenile honu he was looking for. Mark texted Josh to let him know while he still had phone reception.

They continued driving to Hāna, passing the stand of gorgeous rainbow eucalyptus trees and the Garden of Eden at mile marker ten. Waterfalls roared down the mountains and under the old single-lane concrete bridges built in the early 1900s under adventurous circumstances by prisoners from Oahu. Some needed dire repair after years of exposure to the elements and flash flooding. Men in bright orange vests worked along the side of the road, cutting the lush, quick-growing tropical vegetation back from the road.

Mark concentrated on every curve and bump in the road and the oncoming traffic to keep himself and his passengers safe. He couldn't believe he hadn't been back here for more than ten years and swore to return with the kids. That was... if Sienna forgave him.

All these places brought back long-lost memories. The long drive with a beautiful rainforest on one side and steep cliffs and ocean on the other would have been a great opportunity for Mark and Palila to talk about old times, but not with Nalu in the car. She was excited to suddenly have two parents and talked nonstop as they made their way through paradise.

"So, you two used to be in love?" Nalu asked shamelessly.

They glanced at each other, grinning.

"Um, I guess," said Palila. "Things just didn't work out between us, my kaikamahine."

"There was no work for me here, so I had to move away," replied Mark.

"So, that means you still love each other?"

"It's not that easy," replied Palila. Thankfully, Nalu got distracted when they arrived at the sign leading down to the Ke'anae Peninsula. Mark took a left off the Hāna Highway and drove down a bumpy paved road. They passed the famous banana bread stand and waved but didn't stop. A few houses down, they parked along the road and walked down a driveway leading to a small ramshackle house.

Auntie Charlene greeted Palila and then Nalu with a long hug. She looked at Palila, biting her lips, and handed her a big bag of taro and other plants and herbs she had harvested in her yard. Then she handed her another bag with some lilikoi butter and ginger candy. "Suck on the ginger candy when you get nauseous," she said. "It'll settle your tummy."

They sat down at a big wooden table in front of the house to talk and have a cup of coffee. Mark and Nalu walked down to the water on the other side and watched the powerful waves break over the lava rocks.

Auntie Charlene had been friends with Palila's mother since they were children and had been like a real aunt to Palila. Charlene had lived in Ke'anae and Palila's mother, Alana, had lived in Wailuku. They stayed in touch and remained friends as they talked on the phone almost daily. They had even given each other breaks from their children. Palila had spent many weekends in Ke'anae with Charlene and her daughter Tammy. Now, after losing her friend Alana years ago, Charlene was about to lose Palila whom she had watched grow up. Palila was much too young to die, just like her mother had been.

"Don't forget my offer to take care of Nalu," she said.

With tears in her eyes, Charlene waved as Palila, Nalu and Mark drove away. She was planning on visiting Palila in Hāna, but she knew this might be the last time she'd see her. Cancer was evil.

Their next stop was Coconut Glen's. Everyone said hi to their old friend while they got some of his delicious vegan ice cream. Even Palila hadn't seen Glen in forever, so they needed time to catch up. Nalu chased some cats that skittered away from her. Mark looked at his watch. They still had a few miles ahead of them, so they climbed back into the SUV and continued toward Hāna.

As they approached the grocery store, Mark said, "Do you have a fridge at Lani's? Shall we stop and get you some basics?"

"Good idea. Mahalo," Palilo said. "We're staying in a

71

separate studio with its own kitchen and bathroom, so I should get some things to not constantly be on their nerves."

She eased out of the SUV and walked inside the local grocery store. Mark watched her, worried that she looked so weak and fragile. Nalu followed her mom. Mark got out as well to help carry the groceries. At the cash register, there was another big hello, since Palila was an old friend here as well. Lani's grandmother owned the grocery store and had known Palila and Nalu for a long time.

Mark took the bags, and they were on their way to Lani and Max's house right before Hāmoa Beach. They drove through "downtown" Hāna, which was barely a downtown with two more grocery stores, a post office, one hotel, one restaurant, a gas station and some food trucks. That was Hāna. But whoever got charmed by its spell loved it forever.

Cows grazed in the beautiful fields on both sides of the road. They took a left onto Haneo'o Road and drove past Kōkī Beach, a beautiful red sand beach with Alau Island in the distance. Right before Hāmoa Beach, they turned into Max and Lani's driveway. Lani had inherited the property from her Auntie Malani a few years ago. She had been adopted and grew up in the Hudson Valley.

Lani, a beautiful hapa with long dark hair and bright blue eyes in her mid-thirties, was waiting for them. She came out of the house, followed by a girl and a smaller boy, about six and four and greeted the guests.

"E komo mai, welcome."

Since someone had forgotten to close the door properly, two old but feisty basset hounds came running out as well, barking their little hearts out. They jumped up on Palila, Mark and Nalu, almost knocking them over. Lani was beside herself.

"Try to hold them, Nalu and Kai," she shouted, running back into the house for their harnesses and leashes. "I'll be right back, guys! Don't let them run into the road!"

A car sped down the road behind them, and Mark understood Lani's panic. He kneeled and held both dogs, who sniffed him and wagged their tails. They probably smelled the golden retrievers. Lani came back out, smiling at Mark.

"Thanks so much for your help!" She put the harnesses around the hounds and fastened their leashes to them. They tried pulling her toward the street, but she pulled them right back.

She pushed a strand of hair behind her ear.

"I'm Lani, by the way. You must be Mark. And this is Lilly, this is Lucy." She pointed at the lemon basset first, then at the smaller tricolor.

Then she walked over to Palila and gave her a big hug. The kids, Kai, Pablo and Nalu, were already running toward the swing set in the backyard.

They got the luggage out of the car, and Lani led them to a comfortable guesthouse behind the garage.

"We'll drive over to Ana's house tomorrow, okay? You're probably tired and hungry after the long drive," Lani said. Palila nodded. Mark placed the bags of banana bread, veggies and herbs on the counter and Palila explained: "I think most of this is for Ana. We can figure it out later."

Mark looked at his watch. "I should probably get going so I'm not driving all the way in the dark."

"How about some delicious huli chicken from Kōkī Beach before you leave? You must be hungry," said Lani, grinning. She knew nobody could turn down huli huli chicken. "Max is coming home in about five minutes. I'd like you to meet him, too."

Mark realized how hungry he was and thanked Lani. "Sure, I'd love some." Palila put the groceries into the fridge. She was exhausted but upbeat that she and Nalu had such a nice place to stay after the moldy old trailer. Tomorrow, she'd concentrate on herself and some healing energy.

Max, a happy-go-lucky, handsome Hawaiian man in his late thirties, stepped into the guesthouse and greeted everyone. They ate a delicious family dinner on the main house's back porch. Mark made his way back to Wailea just as the sun was setting. He drove down the dark, curvy road onto the Hāna Highway, framed by tall bamboo, monsteras and beautiful African tulip trees.

Meanwhile, Sienna was in the Keys getting upset with Mark for not returning any of her text messages or calls. She was getting on a plane tomorrow morning and was supposed to bring him some gadgets from the turtle hospital. Besides having some questions, it would have been nice to talk to him one more time before her flight.

Chapter 9

Ana Kamealoha, called either Tutu or Auntie Ana by everyone in town, was the oldest elder and healer in Hāna. She was fragile but still actively helping people with wisdom passed on for generations from the ancient Polynesians.

Ana dressed in a long, wide flowery mu'umu'u and fixed her silver-white hair in a bun on top of her head, adding a haku lei with fragrant fresh flowers.

As she did every day, Ana hiked across the street—past Palapala Ho'omau church and Charles Lindbergh's grave—down to the ocean to meditate, pray and watch the sun rise. Ana gave thanks for her community, friends, family and herself. When she was done, the almost 101-year-old used a hand-carved walking stick made of ancient guava wood to make it safely back up the incline toward home. The dense guava wood shimmered gold in the morning light.

Back home, she walked barefoot in her garden to stay connected to the 'āina, the land, which provided her with energy. She still worked on growing and harvesting herbs and vegetables every day. Or just weeding. Her granddaughter Pekelo watched her sometimes and wondered where she found the strength for yard work, but Ana just laughed and said, "Working with the 'āina and making things grow gives me energy."

Herbs hung to dry all over her kitchen. Potions and tinctures lined the shelves along with countless plants, blooms or roots she was chopping or boiling. A stream ran through her backyard providing her with clean and cleansing water from the mountains which she used for all her potions. She washed herself daily with this refreshing water.

She believed in Ho'oponopono, the traditional Hawaiian practice of forgiveness or correction to move things back into balance and maintain harmony with yourself and others. Ana had helped develop a new system of healing based on this ancient spiritual tradition.

Ana strolled through her garden, waiting for Lani to bring Palila over. With a basket under her arm, she passed the more decorative plants: giant heliconias, bird of paradise, all sorts of ginger—variegated, awapuhi, Hawaiian red and torch ginger—as well as gigantic wooded plumerias and orchids everywhere, mounted to trees. Two old wooden benches and a round table invited guests to sit down and enjoy the beautiful surroundings. An enormous blooming specimen-sized Cattleya in a handmade pot sat in the middle of the table. Ana walked up to the well-organized herb and vegetable garden, picked some herbs to make tea and carefully placed them in her basket.

As Ana heard Lani's car drive down the gravel driveway, she walked to the front and greeted her two guests.

"Aloha kakahiaka!" she said. With her kind, wise eyes,

Tutu watched Palila ease out of the car. The drive to Hāna had taken its toll on Palila, and she was sore from the bumpy ride. Without saying a word, Tutu put her hands on Palila's cheeks and looked in her eyes. Tall Palila had to look down because Tutu was almost a head shorter than her. Ana took her hands down and greeted Palila by sharing ha. They pressed the bridges of their noses together while inhaling. Ancient Hawaiians believed this greeting was the key to good health and that it possessed mana (spiritual power). She greeted Lani the same way.

The three of them walked out back and sat down on benches under the heliconia shrubs. Ana described how she would help Palila.

"You know I cannot heal you. I can just help you manage the pain and make you more comfortable. We will try to bring your physical condition into alignment as much as we can, which will also bring your spiritual, emotional and mental condition into alignment and get you ready for the afterlife. We'll be meditating a lot to create peace and relaxation. Do you remember the meditation techniques I taught you years ago?"

Palila nodded. After Palila's mother's death, Ana had taught her deep relaxation breathing techniques which she had never stopped practicing.

"You'll produce a deep state of relaxation and transport yourself to any place you'd like to be."

Palila nodded. She hadn't expected more since she knew wonders didn't happen. She knew her soul was going to leave her body soon, and she had accepted that. What she couldn't accept was the unfairness that her daughter had to grow up without a mother and that she wouldn't be able to watch her daughter grow up. That thought made her cry, and she tried not to think about it right now.

She was still trying to figure out how her afterlife, 'ao'ao mau o ka honua" ("everlasting side of the earth"), would look, where her soul would go, and she hoped Ana might be able to help her with that.

Ana made them tea and served it with avocado chocolate pudding with fresh lilikoi. She didn't eat or serve processed sugar. It was delicious, but Palila didn't have an appetite and barely tried the pudding.

"I think the strenuous drive back and forth might be too much for Palila soon. But I might not have enough space for both Palila and Nalu, so I might have to come over there."

Lani nodded. "We'll play it by ear how Palila feels."

Palila nodded as well. "I enjoyed the drive today very much. It's my favorite part of the Hāna Highway. But yesterday was a bit tiring."

A friendly, middle-aged woman arrived and gave hugs all around.

Lani introduced her. "Palila, this is Konani Kekoa. I met her at the nursey I used to own in the Hudson Valley."

Ana cleaned up the tea dishes and said, "She moved here to study under me. She's been a fine pupil."

"I work part-time at the Hāna Hotel as well. But my true calling is studying the plants and natural medicines used by the ancient Hawaiians. I've studied for years on the Big Island, but I'm learning so much from Ana," Konani added.

She helped Palila get settled on a massage table while Ana

heated the pohaku, stones believed to hold mana, or spiritual power.

"I gathered these stones and the ones you see lining my yard and fire pit from Wailua Nui, an area near Ke'anae. They have healing power and help absorb the pain when heated."

Standing at Palila's head who was lying face down on a massage table, Ana demonstrated how she wanted Konani to do the massages in the future. She centered herself and chanted as she kneaded her hands into Palila's shoulders and upper back, massaged her with long strokes down both sides of her back. Her movements almost reminded of waves covering sand and then pulling back out into the ocean. The motions of hula were also connected. Then Konani took over and gently pulled the smooth hot stones over Palila's back, arms and legs. Palila fell into a deep, relaxed sleep.

"That's what we're trying to achieve. Just relaxation," said Ana, pleased as she watched Palila breathing evenly and peacefully.

Ana and Lani strolled through the garden that Lani loved so much. They stopped underneath the giant plumerias.

"This is so tough on everyone," said Ana, taking Lani in her arms. "How is Nalu handling it?"

"You know her dad suddenly showed up, don't you?

Ana's eyebrows flew up. She hadn't heard yet.

"Where did he suddenly come from? He was never in the picture, was he?"

"No, he didn't even know about Nalu. He just happens to be working on Maui for a few weeks and went to the produce stand. I don't know if he was looking for Palila or if that was a coincidence too."

"Will he want to take Nalu now?"

"I don't know. Maybe it's best for her to be with her dad now. He seems like a very nice guy."

"Where does he live?"

"In Florida."

Ana's eyes grew wide as she placed a hand over her heart. "That would be very far from her friends and family."

"Yeah, I'd miss her terribly too. But I also can't imagine my kids growing up without a father. He has a girlfriend who has three kids and another daughter of his own. She'd be somewhere where not everything reminds her of her makuahine. He's a veterinarian and works at a sea turtle sanctuary. You know how Nalu loves honu. But we're not the ones to decide that. We'll see what Palila wants."

Chapter 10

Sienna's plane landed late in the afternoon. She hauled her heavy luggage down from the baggage claim carousel. Then she walked toward the curb, wondering where Mark was.

Mark rushed up, put a beautiful fragrant lei around her neck and kissed her on the lips. After all the unanswered calls and text messages before her departure, she almost thought he'd forget her here. She sighed, relieved he was there.

"Hey there! What's been going on? I almost thought you didn't want me to come anymore," she said, straight-forward as always.

He avoided looking her in the eyes. His stomach ached over what he had to tell her soon. "I'm sorry, it's been crazy around here. And the time difference didn't help."

"I understand. It just freaked me out a little." She followed him out of the building and into the gorgeous sun and breeze of the trade winds. A few minutes later, the initial awkwardness passed and the usual attraction between Sienna and Mark was back. She could never be mad at him for long. They held hands as she gazed out the window. Endless beaches and ocean flew by on the right, and condos, restaurants and strip malls passed on the left.

He chose the scenic route through Kihei instead of staying on the Pi'ilani highway.

"Look, there's a Starbucks," he said pointing at a building in a small plaza.

She laughed. "I don't want Starbucks. I want real Hawaiian coffee."

Mark had to laugh. "That's exactly what I said to Josh too."

Sienna smiled and put her hand on his.

Soon they arrived in Wailea. Mark headed uphill and took a left into the neighborhood. Sienna beamed. She hadn't been so crazy about the mansions they passed first, but she loved the one they stopped in front of, surrounded by the beautiful overgrown yard.

"Wow, this is nice," she said as they walked across the front porch and entered the house. Arnold Palmer and Ben Hogan came running and greeted them. Sienna laughed as they jumped up, licking her face. She instantly loved the beautiful dogs and couldn't wait to walk them in the morning. Sienna followed Mark as he took her suitcase upstairs to their guestroom. He gave her a kiss.

"I'll give you a few minutes to unpack and take a shower," he said, looking at his watch. "It's five fifteen now. We have a dinner reservation at six p.m. Can you be ready by five forty-five?"

"Sure." She smiled at him and looked around, obviously pleased with the beautiful room.

"I'll be downstairs. I need to make a few phone calls."

She unzipped her suitcase, pulled out some dresses and

shirts that wrinkled easily and hung them in the big walk-in closet. Then she jumped into the refreshing shower and put on a pretty sleeveless dress and a pair of sandals when she was done. She walked into the hallway past another guestroom. Someone had left the door open, and Sienna peeked inside. The bed was unmade, and a few girl's clothes were scattered around.

She walked downstairs and asked Mark, "Is someone else staying in the other guestroom?"

He froze for a second. Had Nalu forgotten some of her things? He lied for the second time.

"Oh, yeah, Josh's daughter stayed here the last two nights."

"I can't wait to meet Josh and his kids."

"You'll love him. He's the nicest guy. We should go."

They pet the dogs one more time, walked out to the car and drove out of the neighborhood. Mark took a left, heading south toward Makena. "I made a reservation at Gannon's. It's right on one of Maui's most beautiful golf courses, and it's supposed to have the most beautiful sunset views."

The sun was already low over the ocean. Sienna marveled at the paradise they passed through. To the west sat a couple more resorts and some upscale neighborhoods with the sparkling ocean peeking out between the buildings. They look a left up a hill into a driveway. Stately monkeypod trees, one of the most cherished trees of Hawaii, framed the driveway leading up the hill. It seemed like thousands of tropical birds were cawing, and invasive coqui frogs were chirping. The sky bathed everything in red, pink and orange. They parked the car and looked back down toward the ocean through the treetops.

A stray cat ran across the parking lot and disappeared under a car.

"Poor homeless kitty," said Sienna.

"I don't think she's that poor," replied Mark. "She probably gets scraps from the restaurant. And look at this beautiful weather all year round!"

Sienna smiled and nodded. The cat reminded her of something.

"Oh, by the way, I promised the girls I'd go to the Cat Sanctuary in Lana'i and take a ton of pictures. That's their latest obsession, so we'd better plan another trip to Maui with the kids."

They stopped in the middle of the driveway and kissed each other passionately. They could barely keep their hands off each other as they walked into the restaurant. They had never been separated this long.

A big wooden bar stretched along the right side of Gannon's open-air dining room, and a terrace faced the ocean, offering patrons a gorgeous view of the sunset.

A hostess walked Mark and Sienna to their table on the terrace and handed them a couple of menus. Their waiter told them about today's specials and recommended some drinks.

They ordered a mai tai for Mark and a lilikoi martini for Sienna. Mark placed his hand on hers, and they sat simply watching and bathing in the glowing symphony of color the setting sun played against the sky and ocean. It couldn't have been a more beautiful late November evening.

Their dinner of local fish and farm-to-table vegetables was delicious. They ate, gazing at the sunset and listening to a guitarist playing romantic Hawaiian tunes in the background. After her second martini, Sienna's eyes became heavy.

"Shall we call it a night? I'm quite tired after the long flight."

Mark hated to ruin her first evening on Maui, but he couldn't wait any longer now that she was here in person. The longer he dragged it out, the worse it would become. *How ironic,* he thought. He had originally planned on proposing to her right now.

"Can we stay a few more minutes? There's something I really need to tell you."

She tilted her head and raised a questioning eyebrow at his reluctant tone. "Sure, what's going on?"

"Trust me, Sienna. What I'm about to tell you was as big a surprise for me as it's going to be for you. It's not very pleasant either."

"What?" She crossed her arms. "Just tell me."

"I ran into an old girlfriend. A girl I dated for about a year before I moved to Florida. Basically, we broke up because I couldn't get a job here, and she was never going to move to Florida with me, so I had to decide between my career and her—"

"And you obviously chose your career."

"Yes. And I was upset at first, but as you know, I moved on, met Isabel and got married and so on. But that's not what this is about. She's dying of cancer."

Sienna swallowed. "I'm so sorry to hear that. How sad." She rubbed her chin, trying to figure out why he was struggling to tell her this.

"And she has a ten-year-old daughter. Who is obviously... mine."

The color faded from Sienna's face. She felt like he had punched her in the gut.

"I'll be right back," she mumbled.

She walked over to the bathroom, turned the cold water on and let the stream run over her wrists. Then she dabbed her face and eyes with some water to cool them off. Sienna wanted to cry but couldn't. She wished he had told her before she had flown halfway across the world. She could've stayed home. Now she was going to spend her time, what was meant to be like a honeymoon, watching Mark say goodbye to an old girlfriend while she babysat the daughter? What was her role supposed to be in this?

A young girl came into the bathroom and looked at her curiously. Sienna still couldn't return to the table, so she walked over to a different area of the terrace where Mark couldn't see her. Leaning against the railing, she stared out into the dark night. An owl hooted, and something chirped noisily. Even though she could barely think, the surroundings and tranquil island music in the background soothed her. She just wanted to sleep and figure out what to do tomorrow.

When Sienna returned to the table, Mark had already had a third drink, which was unusual for him, and taken care of the check. "Sienna, I'm so sorry. It's not my fault. I had no idea about Nalu and just found out myself."

Nalu, thought Sienna. That was all she could think right now.

"I don't know what this will do to us, but your ex-girlfriend and daughter obviously need you right now. I'd like to go back to the house, please, and go to bed. I'm tired." It was not her style to make a scene. She wished she could just storm off and walk back to the house, but she'd have no idea where to go.

"Okay." He got up, and they walked back to the car.

"I guess I should drive. It seems you've had a bit too much to drink."

"Sure." He handed her the keys.

Sienna drove down the driveway and waited for his directions. "Where am I going?" she asked impatiently as she arrived at the main road. He didn't react right away.

He had almost dozed off but straightened up and replied, "Take a right. Then keep going straight until I tell you. We'll be taking another right in about two miles."

After a quiet drive home only interrupted by Mark's directions, Sienna parked in front of the house. They took their shoes off and entered. Josh was waiting for them, sitting on a couch with a glass of wine in his hand and an open bottle on the coffee table.

"Hi Sienna!"

"Hi."

Josh stood and walked over to give her a hug. Sienna stretched out a hand to shake before he could pull her in. Josh gripped her hand and shot a nervous glance at Mark.

"I'm sorry. I'm very tired from the flight. I'm going to head to bed."

"Of course," Josh said as she walked up the stairs.

"Did you tell her, brah?" he asked Mark.

"Yup," he replied. "It didn't go too well."

"Oh, no," said Josh. "I'm sorry, but I guess that was to be expected. Have a glass of wine."

Chapter 11

It was Sienna's turn to suffer from jetlag. She lay wide awake at 3 a.m. Mark snored like a sailor, probably due to the alcohol, which didn't help. She tossed and turned, but finally gave up about half an hour later, put on shorts and a t-shirt and went downstairs.

The dogs loved the change in routine and wagged their tails. Sienna quietly let them out, made herself a cup of coffee, found some tasty banana bread and sat down on the lanai with her laptop. She researched car rentals and found a comparably inexpensive place close by in Kihei that opened at 6 a.m. As soon as they opened, she'd call and have them pick her up and take her to their location so that she'd be independent. Then she researched some local hiking spots that she had planned on walking. She had known from the start that Mark would be working on weekdays and prepared to keep herself busy exploring the island.

An article she had read about photographer Daniel Sullivan and the King's Highway had caught her interest. The King's Highway on Maui was the first road to circumnavigate an entire island. Daniel Sullivan had hiked the entire remains of the King's Highway in nine days and published a book with incredible photography and information about this ancient road, built by the island's indigenous Hawaiian settlers 500 years ago. Sadly, settlement and construction had destroyed most of the King's Highway. One of the most preserved sections was from Keoneoio Bay (La Perouse Bay) to Kaupo, a hiking trail named Hoapili Trail, starting in La Perouse Bay and leading along the coastline to Hanamanioa Lighthouse. Supposedly, it was easy to find blue stones there from the original trail.

Sienna quietly took a shower and got ready for her day. She put on socks and hiking shoes, grabbed her sunscreen and filled her metal water bottle. Right at six, she called Kihei Rent a Car. Mark and Josh were still sleeping peacefully. By the time they woke up at seven, she was gone.

Since she was only here for a week, and she wanted to feel safe driving on lava rock and the Road to Hāna, she splurged and rented a Jeep.

The car rental was smack dab in the middle of Kihei, so she asked the clerk where she could get the best coffee and breakfast. Equipped with lots of recommendations, Sienna decided on a hole-in-the-wall place called "Cinnamon Roll" that had coffee and breakfast sandwiches. Most of the other places weren't even open this early. She got a coffee and an egg croissant to go and walked down to Kameole Beach Park II right across the street.

She sat on a rock wall watching the moon set behind the West Maui Mountains and the night sky turn into the early morning sky. The sun rose on the east side of the island in Hāna, but the sky was still beautiful above the ocean and the

West Maui Mountains. A whale breached in the distance, even though whale season hadn't quite begun. This must have been an early arriver. Sienna waited to see if he'd show himself again, but he didn't.

She walked down the beach toward some lava cliffs sticking out into the ocean, where she realized she could walk from beach to beach. The stress from getting ready for the trip and the flight itself melted away. She thought about Mark's predicament as she walked and realized she couldn't go the whole day without getting a couple things off her chest. She looked at the time on her phone and figured he was probably awake.

"Hello?" Mark sounded groggy, from just waking up or last night's drinking, Sienna couldn't tell.

"Hi, Mark." Sienna paused, taking a break to gather her thoughts.

"I'm sorry —" they said at the same time.

"No, I'm sorry," Sienna said, "about my reaction last night. It's quite a shock."

"You're not the one who should be apologizing."

"Well, people can't choose when they're going to die, and I feel sorry for the little girl. What's her name again?"

"Nalu."

"So, we should try to help Nalu as much as we can. It reminds me of my sister dying and leaving her kids."

"Yeah, I didn't even think about that. They're in Hāna right now, staying with an old friend. I haven't even told you the whole story. They're homeless and have been living in a trailer in a parking lot."

"Wow," Sienna said.

"I'll call and maybe we can go to Hāna this weekend. Can you reschedule the trip to Lana'i on Saturday? I'd hate for you to have to do it by yourself, but maybe you can go on a weekday without me?"

"Yeah. That's fine."

"Okay, well sorry, I need to get to work. There's drama everywhere. Josh and his colleagues think some sea turtles they've been seeing and monitoring on a regular basis are missing. We're having a meeting this morning and might have to drive around and see if we can find any of them. Chances are slim because they might be in the ocean, but you never know."

"Good luck," said Sienna. "I'm going hiking at La Perouse, and I got my own car."

"Great. That's probably a good idea. Maybe you can return it on the weekend to save two days?"

"We'll play it by ear. I called the kids earlier and said hi from you, by the way. Everything is fine, with Sydney too."

"Thanks. Oh, Sienna? Can you meet me around four at the Maui Turtle Rescue? I'll give you a quick tour, and then we can go and have dinner in Lahaina?"

"Sure."

"Okay, see you then. Love you."

"Love you too. Bye."

Mark ended the call and stared into the backyard where the two golden retrievers sniffed something intently. He had to shake off the gloomy thoughts and called Palila, who didn't answer her phone. Then he tried calling Lani.

"Aloha, Mark. Howzit going?" she asked.

"I'm okay. My girlfriend Sienna arrived yesterday. The whole situation was a bit of a shock for her, but she understands. How are things going with Palila and Nalu?"

"As good as they can be. Palila is over at Ana's right now having another massage and resting. She's different every day. Sometimes she seems to have a bout of energy, then she's weak again. Nalu is having a great time with my kids. Kids are so resilient."

"Yeah. Sienna's sister and brother-in-law died in a car accident about eighteen months ago. Sienna had to jump in and become their new mother. It was tough for them, but they're handling it quite well."

"Wow, hats off to Sienna for taking care of them."

"It was a big change for her. She had a career as a lawyer in Boston and gave up her job and moved to the Keys. She still works remotely, though, and for the turtle sanctuary."

"I can't wait to meet her," said Lani. "Are you guys coming over here anytime soon?"

"I have to work at the Maui Turtle Rescue today and tomorrow, but we'll come over for the weekend. That's why I'm calling. I wanted to ask: Can you recommend a good place to stay in Hāna? I know there's only the one hotel in town, and that's out of our price range."

"My dad bought a little cottage across the street from Waioka Pond a couple of years ago. I'll ask him if it's available. If not, my parents have a guest suite you might be able to stay in. They live a few houses down the road from us," she replied. "Is it only for the weekend?"

"Thanks, yes, Friday and Saturday night. I'll have to get

back to the Maui Turtle Rescue on Monday."

"Okay, I'll call you back as soon as I've talked to my mom and dad."

"Mahalo."

After driving down the long and winding road past little beaches and beautiful homes, Sienna arrived in La Perouse Bay where French traveler and scientist La Perouse first set eyes on Maui. The road ended at a small parking lot. She was glad she had the Jeep because she had to drive over harsh lava in order to park. She climbed out, walked down toward the water and stopped at a sign with information about wild dolphins. People stood close to the water, pointing at a pod of dolphins swimming by. Sienna watched the elegant creatures' glistening bodies jump in and out of the water. The sign said:

"...dolphins and whales sleep with only one half of their brain and must consciously decide when to breathe and swim slowly to hold their positions in the water next to their family and friends. To a human swimmer they look like they're awake and swimming, but they're not, and just like us they need undisturbed rest."

The sign asked people not to swim with the dolphins. *Amazing,* thought Sienna. You learn something new every day. Sienna wished she had a pair of binoculars to watch them.

She walked along the trail, surrounded by lava fields on both sides. Even in the early morning, the hot sun beat down on Sienna. She stopped briefly to apply some sunscreen and take a sip of water that would hopefully stay nice and cold in her metal canister. She passed a field of yellow flowers growing on top of the lava and some old stone walls and came up to something that looked like the ruins of an ancient house or temple, maybe of a great chief. Another sign said:

Please stay off cultural sights.

She came up to some wooded areas along the beaches embedded in lava. Goats jumped all over the lava rock and grazed among the shady trees.

Sienna stopped at a little beach in a bay and sat down on a fallen tree. She drank the cool water from her metal bottle as she looked out at the sparkling ocean. More dolphins jumped through the waves. They seemed to be everywhere. Her thoughts wandered back to Palila and her daughter who would be alone once her mother was gone. She thought about how distraught Lilly, Lindsey and Leo had been after their parents had died. This woman had to prepare herself to die, knowing she'd leave her daughter all alone in the world. Sienna's eyes filled with tears. *She must be happy that Mark showed up,* Sienna thought. All she could do was try to help.

Sienna tried to shake the sad feelings off and enjoy her vacation. The sad part in Hāna would come soon enough.

She walked on the shady trail until it opened into lava fields along steep cliffs leading down to the ocean. Sienna took out a baseball cap, putting it on to shade her face. A honu swam along the cliffs two hundred feet below her.

The path became harder as the sharp lava rocks grew bigger. Sienna stepped from rock to rock to avoid spraining an ankle. She wondered if she was walking on the ancient King's Highway. She couldn't see the blue rocks it was famous for but assumed there might be new layers of lava from more recent volcanic outbreaks covering the ancient road. She asked a couple walking by about the King's Highway, and they said,

"It's right here!"

She thought of long-gone generations of Hawaiians and warriors who had walked on the same road, protecting their island and trading goods. Other than her own steps on the rocks and occasionally the ocean below her, an eerie silence enveloped the trail. Endless fields of lava spread toward the southern tip of the island ahead of her.

In the distance, across the ocean, she saw another island, maybe Kahoolawe, the island that was uninhabited due to lack of fresh water. It had become a training ground for the US military after WWII. She had read in a historical novel that cattle swam all the way across the channel from Maui to Kahoolawe when people tried to make the island habitable. It seemed much too far.

Sienna finally spotted Hanamanioa "Lighthouse", her goal, in the distance. It wasn't really a lighthouse, just a thirty-foot mast with a beacon at the top. With nothing but blue water ahead and desolate lava rock behind her, it felt like she'd reached the end of the world. She sat down on the concrete foundation, enjoying the cool trade winds and the views. This was so different than the touristy areas of Maui in Kihei and Wailea Sienna had seen so far. She liked what she saw and felt the spiritual effect that Maui had on people.

Chapter 12

Billionaire Julian Jensen was an American self-made man. The youngest son of farmers in the midwest, he barely graduated from high school and never went to college. He had started his career as a production assistant in a small TV station and had worked his way up to a newscaster, TV executive, producer of several successful TV shows and finally owner of several TV stations. After being diagnosed with Multiple Sclerosis, he had retired to Maui a few years ago and purchased a stately mansion near La Perouse. Having become quite a recluse and with tourism in the Hawaiian islands at a peak, Maui quickly became too busy for Jensen. He moved to a waterfront mansion in southwest Lana'i which was much more remote than Maui and only accessible by ferry or private planes and a few charters. After being diagnosed with his condition ten years ago and only having some episodic flares for a few years, Jensen was now in a pattern of steady deterioration. He had to walk on a cane, used a wheelchair at home and didn't have much longer to live. Luckily, he could afford to keep a team of physical therapists and a nurse on staff and remain as comfortable as possible. There was one thing he longed for but money couldn't buy: An 'aumakua.

In Hawaiian mythology, an 'aumakua is a family god that may manifest in form of an owl, shark, whale or sea turtle. Hawaiians believed that deceased family members would transform into 'aumakua and watch over them and protect them, giving them strength and guidance, warning them of danger and rewarding worthy people with prosperity in the after life.

Jensen couldn't take his fortune with him, but he had become obsessed with having his own 'aumakua who'd protect and take care of him after his death. He certainly lacked spirituality and liked to joke around that he was rich enough that he could just buy a honu as his own 'aumakua. A big mistake, maybe a joke, he had just made on public TV on the local news as he was interviewed on his property, a well-working organized farm and tropical gardens that made Jensen independent from the food supply chain.. The coup de gras was Jensen's very own enclosed aquatic paradise. He had copied ancient Hawaiian fishponds where he raised edible fish and housed coral to grow his own private reef. His dream was adding a Hawaiian honu to his collection of local aquatic animals – or attracting them to come and stay on his beach.

Most people watching this live broadcast on TV, especially Hawaiians, didn't think this was a joke or funny at all. Honu didn't belong to anyone. They were sacred and protected and certainly not for sale. Even the reporter interviewing him today was appalled.

"Mr. Jensen, are you aware of what you just said? Our Hawaiian community is already bombarding us with angry phone calls. Honu are sacred and not for sale."

"I was joking, man," Jensen replied but nobody believed him at this point, and the show was interrupted for a commercial break. He had made that that joke one too many times.

Chief Inspector O'Shen Larson with the Maui PD, banged her coffee down a bit too abruptly. The coffee splattered all over the table and the floor. She turned the TV off and scoffed to herself as she reached for a paper towel and wiped up the coffee. "What does that arrogant jerk think he's doing? He's not going to be able to set foot out his front door anymore soon."

Julian Jensen's "joke" on public television caused a chain reaction of people fearing for their beloved honu on Maui as well as on Lana'i. Countless calls came in to the Maui PD from people who thought honu they saw on a regular basis were missing. Strangers and tourists on the beaches observed each other as they took harmless photos of themselves with honu, even when keeping the appropriate distance. The neighborhood watches were activated and started working, patrolling the beaches to protect Maui's honu.

Right after arriving at the office that morning, Kaipo answered a call from a local fisherman in a neighborhood near Olowalu. Neighbors were alarmed that a few honu were missing that usually hung out on the beach. Since everyone was on high alert due to Julian Jensen's "joke" on TV this morning, Josh decided to check it out and talk to some of the locals and regulars.

"Hey, we really haven't had much of a chance to talk in private. Would you care to join me?" Josh asked Mark.

Mark had just finished demonstrating another laser treatment on a honu with fibropapillomatosis and was answering some emails from Florida. He closed his laptop and jumped up to join Josh.

"Sure, I can send this email later."

"Let's take my car. I can drop you off here on the way back." He looked at his watch. "Shall we grab some sandwiches to go first? Or wait, let's have lunch in Pai'a when we're done."

Mark nodded. "Sounds like a plan."

They stepped out of the small office and almost bumped into Nora who was taking care of some honu in the courtyard basins. Dressed in designer clothes and expensive earrings, Nora didn't look like an intern at the Maui Turtle Rescue. She looked at Josh, blinking her big blue eyes and asked, "Josh, can we talk about Hilo when you're back? The honu with the shark bite?"

Josh, who was still heartbroken about his recent divorce and had no interest in Nora whatsoever besides as a colleague, ignored her flirtatious behavior and replied matter-of-factly: "Of course. Is she okay?"

"The wound looks infected. I'd just like a second opinion."

Josh looked at his watch. The caller in Olowalu was waiting. "We have to go right now, why don't you rinse it with some more betadine for now, and I'll take a look later when I'm back."

"Okay, thanks." She batted her long eyelashes at Josh and

Mark before they left.

"Dude, what's up with that intern," said Mark to Josh as they walked toward the parking lot and climbed into Josh's SUV. Josh rolled his eyes. "It gets a little annoying, but I just ignore it. Besides that, she does a really good job."

"So, what's up with Sienna?" Josh asked to change the subject. "Has she cooled off at all?"

"Yeah, she called me this morning. We apologized to each other. She understands there's nothing I could have done."

"Good, I'm glad," said Josh. "What's Palila's prognosis? I can't even imagine. And does she expect you to take Nalu? Did you even discuss that yet?"

"She doesn't have more than a couple of weeks to live."

"Wow, I'm so sorry, that's horrible."

"I haven't even been able to think about the situation with Nalu. Of course, I'd take her, but I'm not sure if Palila would want her to leave Maui. That's why we broke up in the first place. She and her family would've never left this island."

Josh nodded. He remembered what happened back then.

An old fisherman waited for them at Olowalu Beach. He was there every morning and had called the hotline.

Shady milo trees lined the beach. A tree favored by King Kamehameha, it was considered sacred by early Polynesians. Its wood was used to make beautiful bowls and carvings, the bark for cordage, the fruit to make dyes, the leaves and flowers were edible. A big variety of fruit trees grew here as well.

Tents, tentalows and a few cabins were off to the side in the camping area. People snorkeled in the shallow water with Olowalu's unique reef, a "mother reef" sending out polyps and seeding new reefs as far as Lana'i and Molokai. Honu and manta rays used it as a cleaning station, feeding and socialization area. Fish ate the algae off sea turtles' shells and literally cleaned them.

Josh parked. They climbed out of the SUV and greeted the fisherman.

"Aloha, Kevin? Are you the one who called this morning? I'm Josh from the Maui Turtle Rescue, and this is my co-worker Mark," Josh introduced himself and Mark. The middle-aged man smiled, his face wrinkling heavily from sun exposure and premature aging.

"Aloha. Mahalo for coming. Let me show you where the honu usually are. We're not sure but we think they might have been disturbed or taken," replied Kevin.

"Did you hear what Julian Jensen said on the news this morning?" asked Josh.

"Yes, and that's making everyone especially nervous," replied Kevin as he led them toward the sandy beach where they spotted a big honu basking in the sun.

He stopped and pointed at the honu. "See where he is? There's usually five or six honu right in that area, and I haven't seen them in days. Several of my colleagues and their families who hang out here have been saying the same thing."

Josh ground his teeth as they walked along the beach. He had heard about poaching incidents on the Big Island years ago, but it had never happened on Maui since he worked here. Was this a possibility? Was indeed someone trying to steal a honu for Jensen?

"Just to be safe, we'll inform the Endangered Species

Branch at NOAA, the National Oceanic and Atmospheric Administration and I'll talk to my contact with the local police department," said Josh as they walked back to the parking lot.

"Thanks for making us aware of this, Kevin. We need to take these things seriously, especially after what Jensen said on TV this morning," said Josh. "I'll be in touch. We'll be looking for volunteers for the watch group. Maybe you can start asking around?"

"Our neighborhood watch is already working around the clock."

"I'll call my contact with the local police right away, and with NOAA. We need to react to this fast. Mahalo for calling us, Kevin."

"Mahalo," Kevin said and walked back to his truck and boat trailer.

As they headed back toward Pai'a, Josh said, "Wow, if any of the honu were stolen or even disturbed, that's serious. I'd be curious if we find the same situation at Ho'okipa Beach or other locations."

"Yeah, I haven't heard of a case of poaching in years."

"Poachers could be stealing them to sell them to aquariums or zoos. Sadly, some places would rather buy from poachers than go the legal way, which is much more expensive," said Josh. "Let me call my friend O'Shen Larson with the local police. She's probably going to tell me that it falls in NOAA's jurisdiction, but I'd like the local police to keep their eyes open as well. I've heard they cooperate with NOAA in lots of situations."

He picked up his phone and dialed a number in his

contacts.

"Kahului Police Headquarters. This is Chief Inspector Larson," O'Shen answered. Her voice always sounded intimidating with strict guttural German undertones, as her mother was German, and she had spent time in Germany.

"Aloha, O'Shen. This is Josh Templeton with the Maui Turtle Rescue. Do you remember me?" They had met at a few Maui Turtle Rescue events and a couple honu rescues when the police got involved.

"Of course, I remember you. Aloha, Josh! Howzit going? What can I do for you?"

"My team has been noticing that one of the honu we track and see in the same location on a regular basis isn't showing up. In addition to that, we received a call today from a local fisherman in Olowalu saying that some of the honu that usually hang out there haven't been around either. I might sound paranoid, but I wanted to ask if you could have the beaches patrolled a bit more often."

"Well, did you hear what Julian Jensen said on the local news this morning? Our phones have been ringing off the hook with people calling about honu they think are missing. Please take what the fisherman says seriously but also with a grain of salt..."

"I know what he said, but I think due to that we have to be even more responsive to these calls by the public."

"Good point," replied O'Shen. "Well, I agree with you that we should take this fisherman seriously. And we will make an exception and be on high alert because of what Jensen said. Normally, we wouldn't be able to do anything until a crime has actually been committed, but the situation is different. We have to AVOID a crime involving honu. Do you want me to send a couple of officers out there? We can check out the beach and talk to some people in the area."

"Yes, and maybe we can organize a watch group to keep an eye out."

"Great idea. So, the main area you're concerned about is Olowalu Beach?"

"Yes and Ma'alaea Harbor. Those seem to be the areas concerning us most, at least right now. My colleague Mark and I are currently on our way to Ho'okipa Beach. Say hi, Mark. You're on speakerphone, O'Shen."

Mark and O'Shen both greeted each other.

Josh continued: "There seem to be some honu missing there too. It's hard to tell. They could just be going somewhere else or swimming in the ocean. But honu are usually creatures of habit."

"I'll tell my team to keep an eye out for anything suspicious. And I'll send a couple of officers out to Olowalu in an undercover vehicle at random times."

"That would be great. Thanks, O'Shen."

"Please keep me informed if we need action on other beaches. And call Jerry with NOAA. They need to be informed. Although, I'm sure they're getting a ton of calls already too..."

Josh thanked O'Shen again and ended the call. Mark asked: "I've heard about this Julian Jensen guy. Isn't he the super wealthy film producer who has MS?

"Yeah, he lives on Lana'i and is super arrogant despite his illness. He thinks he owns or can buy everything, even honu.

That is so disrespectful, especially to the Hawaiians. Honu are sacred to them."

They had almost arrived in Pai'a and changed the subject. As usual in the busy little beach town, traffic was stop and go.

"I'll have to come here with Sienna. She'd love this," said Mark as they drove through the busy surfing town. They drove out of Pai'a and along a couple miles of beautiful coastal road with oceanfront houses, shops, a cemetery and a Buddhist temple, until they reached Ho'okipa Beach Park. A chain closed off the road leading down to the beach. Josh stopped in front of the chain and put a sign identifying him as a Maui Turtle Rescue member on the dashboard. Mark got out of the truck to unhook the chain so Josh could drive through, then closed it behind him.

They drove down the bumpy road to some public bathrooms and parked the truck in front of the beach.

Mark climbed out of the truck. He breathed deeply as he watched the surfers waiting in the ocean for the next wave.

This was where he had first surfed as a rookie and gotten hammered by the merciless waves. Palila had kept him from giving up and eventually taught him how to surf. Josh remembered too. He had witnessed it all.

"Lots of memories here, brah, right?"

"Yes, crazy. It seems like that was in a different life."

Josh clapped a hand on Mark's shoulder. He walked down to the east side of the beach leading up to the observation area and parking lot. Mark followed him. Josh stopped short. Where there were usually twenty honu basking in the sun, there were only three. His trained eyes checked for the Maui Turtle Rescue tattoo. None of the three had it. That meant that the approximately ten honu the Maui Turtle Rescue kept tabs on were either missing, not coming for some reason, or they just happened to not be there right now. It was a tough call.

"We should keep a sharp eye on this beach as well," Josh said. "I'll call O'Shen back and ask if she can have it observed too."

Chapter 13

Sienna sat at Hanamanioa Lighthouse looking out at the ocean when a lonely hiker approached her from the other direction. He had obviously been swimming in the bay a hundred feet below since he carried a rolled-up towel under his arm. His salt-and-pepper hair was still wet. Tired from climbing back up onto the main trail, he stopped and took a sip of water out of a metal water bottle. He saw Sienna sitting there, her auburn hair glowing in the sun, and walked a few steps closer. She was embarrassed he'd caught her watching him, but he talked as if they were old friends.

"Water's beautiful. You should go for a dip too, it's really refreshing."

"Honestly, I don't think I have the energy to climb down there today after the hike out here. I just flew in yesterday from the east coast, and I feel my jet lag returning after being awake since three a.m. It does look beautiful and refreshing though."

"Where did you fly in from?"

"Florida. Actually, Miami."

"Ouch, that's a long flight. And you're here all by yourself?"

"No, I'm here with my boyfriend, but he's working at the

Maui Turtle Rescue, so I have a lot of spare time on my hands," she replied, smiling.

"I'm Tom, by the way. Tom Brantley." He stretched out his hand to shake hers.

Sienna laughed. "No way! That's my last name too. I'm Sienna Brantley."

"Well, I hope we're not related," he said flirtatiously, happy to have a beautiful woman accompany him on the long hike back to the car.

"It's actually my ex-husband's last name," Sienna explained as they walked through the lava fields along the coast. "I've been thinking of taking my maiden name back."

"And what's that? You must admit that Brantley is quite a nice name."

"My maiden name is Anderson. I actually like that name too."

"So, where is your ex-husband from? Do you know any Brantleys in the Hudson Valley?"

"I don't think so. He's from Boston, and all his family is there, as far as I know. We were only married for a short time though. I never met anyone except his parents. He's a single child."

"What's his first name?"

"Sean."

"Nope. Don't know any Sean."

Uncomfortable with the personal line of questioning, Sienna changed the subject. "So, what brings you here?"

"Well, that's a long story, but I guess we have time, right?" He grinned, pointing at the long hike ahead of them. "My wife

Katherine was Hawaiian. She died last year of ovarian cancer."

Sienna listened up. What a coincidence. Palila had ovarian cancer as well.

"I'm sorry to hear that," she said.

"My twin daughters grew up on Maui, but we've lived on the west coast for the past few years because of work. My daughters both just left for college. I'm an empty nester and accepted a job offer in Kihei. To be honest with you, I'm having a hard time living by myself for the first time after so many years. And I missed Maui, so I decided to move back when I got the offer. It's not easy with the skyrocketing prices. I came a few days early to clear my mind and tour some houses before I start working. They're putting me up in a condo for a month."

"May I ask what you do?"

"I'm a family lawyer, but I'm going to be working with a non-profit organization assisting Hawaiians in danger of losing their property because of all the rich investors scooping up the land. There are some new laws that help kanaka, that means indigenous Hawaiians. Not many people are aware of them. The locals have significant tax exemptions, but most don't even know about them, so they don't apply."

"That sounds great. I'm a lawyer too, by the way."

"Wow, so many coincidences. We must be related somehow," he laughed. "What specialty?"

"I work for a firm for international law in Boston. Although right now I just freelance because my sister and brother-in-law in the Keys both died and left me two nieces and a nephew. I had to move down there."

He looked at her, his mouth gaping open. Amazing what

people had to go through. "Wow, I'm sorry to hear that."

She pointed toward another pod of spinner dolphins. "It was and is still awful that my nephew and nieces lost their parents so early. But it also gave me another outlook on life. I was probably going to continue living my single life, working eighty hours a week until I died of a heart attack one day, a lonely wealthy boring old lady, living on Boston Common. Now my life is messy, colorful and full of love. I can't imagine being without those kids anymore, as tough as it is sometimes."

He smiled. What a sympathetic beautiful woman.

"I totally get that. My entire life revolves around my daughters. Even though they drive me nuts sometimes — or let's say mostly."

"I can see that," she replied. "Do you have any photos of them? They must be gorgeous."

He got his phone out and showed her some recent photos of his beautiful hapa teenage daughters, half Hawaiian, half Caucasian.

"Do you know what they did last year for Christmas? They met this teenage girl on vacation who was pregnant and hid her in a barn close to my sister-in-law's house in Hāna where we were staying at the time. You might have read about it in the news. She was missing for days."

Sienna looked at him with big eyes. "No, I didn't hear about it. That's crazy! Did the pregnant girl and the baby end up being okay?"

"She had the baby right there in the barn! Thank goodness an old healer lives right there. My daughters finally went and got her when the baby was coming and they all started panicking."

"What a story. They're gorgeous, but I can also see they might be quite mischievous. They remind me of The Parent Trap in Hawaiian," Sienna replied laughing.

"Haha, that's true. Do you have a picture of your nieces and nephew? It's one boy and two girls?"

"Yes, they're seventeen, twelve and seven now. And the crazy thing is that my boyfriend Mark also has a seven-year-old daughter." She was about to tell Tom about Mark's "new" daughter and ex-girlfriend but hesitated. It was nice to meet Tom and forget about that situation for a while.

He didn't notice her hesitation. "Wow, you've got quite the Brady Bunch there."

They walked silently next to each other for a while, enjoying the beautiful surroundings. The heat and rough terrain made it a tough hike. Sienna slipped and almost got her ankle stuck between two rocks. Tom stretched his hand out to grab hers. There was an embarrassing moment as their hands touched, and they felt the tension between them. Sienna's cheeks grew hot as she snatched her hand back. Tom cleared his throat and looked away. They kept walking in silence. The path finally turned into an easier trail of smaller pebbles, then eventually sand in the wooded, shady area leading along little bays and beaches.

"This would be a great opportunity to go for a dip. Do you have your bathing suit with you?" asked Tom.

"No," said Sienna regretfully. The water did look refreshing. "But I should get back anyhow. I need to go back and answer some emails before I meet my boyfriend for an early dinner."

"That's too bad," laughed Tom, flirting a little. He really found Sienna intriguing, but he wasn't a homewrecker and hoped she could just be friends with him.

Sienna didn't know how to answer. She really liked Tom too. He was attractive, and Sienna wasn't sure if the situation might become dangerous if she continued talking to him. Could a man and woman who were attracted to each other on some level just be friends?

"Well, I should get back to the car, it looks like we're almost there," she said, then tried to change the subject to something neutral. "By the way, do you know anything about the King's Highway? It's supposed to be here, but I didn't really see the blue rocks that are supposed to be in the middle of the trail."

"I'm not sure myself," he replied. "As far as I know, the original trail is further inland, but some parts of the trail we just hiked might belong to the King's Highway too."

Tom didn't want to let Sienna go without the chance of seeing her again. Carefully, without being too obvious that he liked her, he said, "I really enjoyed hiking with you. If you don't have any plans yet for tomorrow, I have a trip to Lana'i planned and would love for you to join me. No strings attached. Just friends. We'll rent a Jeep and drive around a little. I'm meeting a friend in Lana'i City around noon, but it'll be quick, and you could check out the galleries or have a coffee in the meantime."

Sienna liked the proposal, but she wasn't sure if it was a good idea to spend an entire day with a stranger. She thought about how she would feel if Mark went to Lana'i to spend the whole day with a woman he'd just met hiking.

"I'm not sure about tomorrow yet. I did have plans to maybe go hiking up the Waihee Ridge Trail, but Lana'i sounds tempting too. Why don't I let you know tonight? When does the ferry leave in the morning?"

"At six thirty." He got a Post-it note out of his car, wrote down his phone number and handed it to her. "Give me a call. We'd take the ferry and be back in Lahaina by six thirty. I'll be your tour guide," he said with a smile.

Tom seemed like a nice guy, but was he too nice? Sienna wasn't up for a flirt, but maybe a fun, carefree day before meeting Palila and Nalu on Friday was just what she needed.

Chapter 14

After her treatments at Ana's house the previous day, Palila was having one of her more energetic mornings. Some days she was in so much pain she couldn't get out of bed. Some days she felt almost normal but knew she'd suffer the next day if she overdid it.

As the sun rose, she and Nalu walked down to Hāmoa Beach, her favorite beach, praised by author James Michener as the most beautiful in the Pacific for a good reason. The beach's perfect crescent shape was surrounded by lush greenery and hills. Some great frigatebirds hanging out here fluttered across the gray sky.

Nalu, mature beyond her years and always worried about her mother, walked closely next to her to support her if she became faint or stumbled. The beach was just a few hundred yards down the road, but there was no sidewalk. A couple cars filled with locals on their way to work passed them, but it was too early for the steady stream of tourists that would be driving by later in the day.

"Nalu, you should be working on your school curriculum, not coming with me. School is important," said Palila.

"It's okay, Mama, I can start later. Nobody goes to school

this early. You know I get all the work done in two hours. Regular school is like six hours. You're just waiting for the slower kids the whole time. I've been helping Kai with her homework."

Palila nodded. She was so proud of her smart daughter and knew she'd do fine in life, whatever happened.

They stopped at a stand of wooded plumeria trees overlooking the crescent-shaped beach and roaring ocean beneath them. Yellow-white blooms torn off by the wind sprinkled the ground.

Nalu picked up a plumeria and stuck it behind her mother's ear. They smiled at each other and stood for a long while, looking down at the ocean. Palila, struck with a dizzy spell, sat down on the stone wall lining the road. Beads of sweat appeared on her upper lip, and her breathing was labored. Nalu followed her and asked, "Are you okay, Mom?"

Palila got up, determined to make it to the beach without help. "Yes, I'm okay. Let's walk down the stairs." She used all her strength to walk down the flight of concrete steps leading to the beach, holding on to the metal railing on one side and Nalu on the other. They were the only people here this early.

The sun, still sitting low and perfectly positioned in the east, shone through the large waves. In the spray, they could see fragments of a rainbow.

"This is called a sea spray bow. It's a refraction and reflection of the low sunlight hitting the water droplets blown by the wind from the breaking waves," Palila said.

Nalu nodded. They took off their slippahs, left them by the shower and walked through the soft light-brown sand down to the shoreline.

The excitement of seeing the sea spray bow gave Palila some new mana, spiritual energy. She closed her eyes and took a deep breath. The sea spray bow had disappeared when she opened her eyes again. Peace overcame her in this spiritual place. This was where she wanted her ashes spread. She'd talk to Lani about it later.

Palila waded through the cool soothing ankle-deep water. Nalu ran ahead, turned around and watched her footprints disappear as they filled up with water. Palila's eyes brimmed with tears as she watched Nalu. Nalu still had the priceless ability to be lost in the moment discovering the simple wonders of physics and nature. They walked toward the hills on the west side of the beach. Palila sat down on a weather-beaten branch under the shady trees and continued watching Nalu play in the shallow water.

She looked up the hill next to her. The entire area between Hāmoa Beach and Waioka Pond—the Makaalae-Mokae lands—held generations of Hawaiian history. It was full of iwi, the buried bones of ancestors, possibly even some of royalty. A few years ago, the same ruthless developer, Joseph McAllen, who bought Palila's foreclosed house, had tried to buy this land and build oceanfront condos. The people of Hāna had stopped him and had purchased the land to preserve and maintain it. It was now forbidden to subdivide and develop the land. Palila sighed. Sometimes the good won, but Joseph McAllen was still buying properties all over the island and turning it into a concrete jungle. She cringed thinking of what would become of the beautiful old plantation she had lost that had been in her family for generations. Maybe that was killing her...

On the other side of the beach, someone walked down the steps, a surfboard under his arm. The man crossed the beach without stopping, jumped chest first onto the board, getting him over the first wave break, and paddled out to deeper water. Palila could tell he was on a mission and only had so much time to get in as much surfing as possible.

It reminded her of when Nalu was a baby. Her mother would watch her for a while in the morning, and she made it out to the ocean, determined to keep up with her surfing. Oh, what would she give to be able to stand on a surfboard just one more time and conquer the powerful waves! She used to be so strong and remembered the adrenaline coursing through her veins when she rode a wave. Her bones were brittle now, her muscles had disappeared, and her joints were in constant pain. Cancer was winning. Palila had gone surfing with Nalu a few times and hoped she'd gain interest. Nalu noticed the surfer as well and stood in the knee-deep water, watching him with riveted attention.

She yelled, "Mama, look! Just like you used to surf!"

Palila nodded and watched the man wait for a perfect wave, paddle quickly and then jump up to crouch on the surfboard and glide across the surface of the water. He was a good surfer and rode the fierce waves like a pro but experienced his share of beatings from the merciless ocean. Palila and Nalu cheered him on and suffered with him when a big wave crashed over him.

Finally, he was tired or out of time and casually rode a wave all the way back to shore. He made his way out of the water and discovered Nalu standing there watching him. He walked toward her. Palila recognized Lani's husband, Max.

"Aloha, Nalu, are you here all by yourself this early?"

"No, my mom's back there. We went for a walk, but she needs to rest. She gets tired."

He looked over at the trees and waved to Palila. She slowly got up and walked closer.

"You did really great, Max," she said. "You must surf quite a bit."

"Well, you probably know yourself how that goes, between work and the kids. I'm lucky if I get to come out here once a week. But Lani and I take turns getting our breaks."

He tousled Nalu's hair. Max knew what a fabulous surfer Palila had been. *Not being able to surf anymore must be so painful,* he thought.

"Hey, why don't you get your swimsuit on later and you can sit on the board while I hold it. And Nalu, how about a lesson later this afternoon when I get home from work? I was planning on going out with Kai and Paolo today."

Both of their faces lit up. He knew exactly how to make their day. They all walked back together, passing the new sign that locals had set up on the beach:

"Cultural Preservation Area

WAHI KAPU (sacred place)
Mōkae Cove – Hāmoa Beach
Nā iwi kūpuna (bones of our ancestors) are preserved and safeguarded beneath these grounds.
Nā iwi kūpuna are recognized with rock mounds to ensure their protection.

By entering this wahi kapu, you have agreed to respect nā iwi
kapūna that remains here.
Mahalo
Ua Mau ke Ea o ka ʻĀina i ka pono
The Life of the Land is Perpetuated in Righteousness"

Chapter 15

O'Shen Larson had requested the entire department attend a meeting in the conference room at one p.m. Some of the officers wanted to go on their lunch breaks, but no one dared skip the meeting. O'Shen could be quite a tyrant. There would be hell to pay if people had dumb excuses for not showing up.

"Thanks for coming, everyone," she started the meeting. "The Maui Turtle Rescue has brought to my attention that we might be dealing with a case of honu poaching here on the island. I guess you've all heard about the Julian Jensen incident in the meantime, so it might be a false alarm. I know we usually wouldn't be swinging into action until a crime has been committed, but I'm making an exception due to what Jensen said and because of the honus' special status on the island. We need to be on high alert."

Everyone mumbled. There hadn't been any poaching cases on the island in years. Everyone loved the Hawaiian honu and knew they were protected and a big part of the culture.

"If Jensen's intending on having someone steal a honu for him, that would be a heinous crime. The last recorded honu poaching case in Hawaii was on the Big Island in 2004. One of the honu that Maui Turtle Rescue tracks on a regular basis has actually not been seen in a while. Let's hope we're just being paranoid, and he's hanging out somewhere else."

The officers shook their heads.

O'Shen continued. "The beaches so far involved are Olowalu Beach and Ho'okipa. My contact at Maui Turtle Rescue, Josh Templeton, and his team are checking further beaches as we speak. We're going to have undercover officers observe these beaches around the clock. Also, I'd like volunteers to hang out at the beaches undercover as fishermen and maybe find out more." She pointed at an officer. "Officer Thomas, set up a schedule and have officers sign up. It needs to be 24/7."

Officer Thomas nodded. "Sure thing, Inspector Larson."

"Check the harbors and the airports in Kahului and Kapalua and even Hāna. We need to keep anybody from taking them off island. Check the cruise ships. Honu are big and not easy to hide. Any more ideas or input?"

Nobody had any other ideas, so she ended the meeting.

"I'll be Maui Turtle Rescue's contact, so keep me updated with any news on this case. Officer Thomas, email me the schedule for observing Olowalu and Ho'okipa Beach ASAP. Mahalo."

After everyone had left, O'Shen walked into her office and closed the door. She called Josh.

"Any news from Ho'okipa Beach?"

"There are certainly less honu than usual, as far as I can tell from going there once. Something or somebody must be disturbing them."

"Okay. We're setting up a schedule right now for 24/7 observation of both beaches. Also, we'll have an undercover cop go to Olowalu Beach disguised as a fisherman tomorrow morning. All this information is strictly confidential. Don't even discuss it with your coworkers."

"Got it."

"Thanks, we'll keep you posted. Please let us know if any more beaches become involved."

"Will do. There are usually quite a lot of honu on the Kihei beaches as well. I'll check those myself on the way home today."

"Mahalo," said O'Shen.

———————◗◉◖———————

Josh and Mark drove back to Maui Turtle Rescue after a nice lunch in Pai'a. Josh glanced at Mark.

"Didn't you say you're taking Sienna to Duke's for dinner after work? Any way you could take her for a sightseeing tour up to Napili Bay and check on the honu up there? There are usually quite a few on those beaches as well."

"Sure, I love that area," replied Mark. "Maybe I'll take her to Sea House instead of Duke's. I've never been there."

Josh thought for a second. "What's today, Thursday? There's usually a good slack key guitar player on Thursdays, so you might get lucky."

"Sounds great, I'll check it out."

———————◗◉◖———————

At 4 p.m., Sienna parked her rental Jeep in the Maui Turtle

Rescue parking lot and walked up to the row of low buildings. She assumed the Turtle Rescue was in the back, so she headed that way as she texted Mark. *I'm here, where's your office?*

Coming out to meet you, he replied.

He stepped out of a door, and they almost bumped into each other.

"Hey!" Mark took the opportunity and gave her a hug and a kiss. "You look great," he said, looking at the Hawaiian dress she had changed into. "Is that dress new?"

"Yes, it is," she replied. "I just stopped in this little shopping plaza in Kihei to buy some gifts for the kids and couldn't resist when I saw it."

"I can't wait to hear about the rest of your day." He led her into the small courtyard with a few sea turtles in basins. "This is it," he said, pointing at the courtyard. He opened another door and walked inside.

"And this is my temporary office. Let me just close my laptop, and then I'll introduce you to everyone."

Kaipo and Nora knocked and stepped into the office, apologizing when they saw Sienna.

"Oh, we're so sorry, we didn't mean to interrupt," said Nora. "We just wanted to let you know we got a call about a honu stuck between some rocks near Makena Beach. Josh is going with us and told us to tell you not to bother, since you're going in the opposite direction."

"Are you guys sure?" asked Mark.

"Yes, three people are plenty, probably even two. They get stuck quite often in the lava rock down there. They hang out by the rocks at high tide to feed on the algae. Then when the tide recedes, they can't get out anymore. We just give them a lift and a push, and they're on their way. It's not that dramatic. Well, sometimes they dig themselves deeper into the crevices in the rocks, and they're really stuck, but we can handle that. We always do," replied Nora, smiling.

Mark nodded.

"By the way, Nora and Kaipo, this is my girlfriend, Sienna."

They all said hi, and Nora and Kaipo left.

"Well, that's basically it," said Mark. "It's only Josh, Kaipo, the vet tech, and Nora, the intern, and a few freelance vets and some volunteers who are on call around the clock to assist with chores and take emergency calls."

"They seem nice."

Mark looked at his watch. "Okay, let's go! We still have a good two and a half hours of sunlight. I hope it's okay with you, Josh asked me to go to some beaches in the Napili Bay area and count the honu hanging out there. There's a real issue now with the missing honu. Someone might be trying to steal them."

"Oh, no, of course I don't mind," Sienna replied. "That's terrible. Who would do that?"

"Someone who doesn't care about honu and wants to make a lot of money. They're probably worth a lot of money on the black market. Or billionaire Julian Jensen. Did you hear about what he said on TV this morning?"

"No, I haven't. What did he say?"

"That guy is so dumb. He said he wants his own personal honu as his own 'aumakua, which in the Hawaiian culture is a spiritual protector of someone's family."

Sienna nodded. "I've heard about that."

As they walked out to the parking lot, Sienna asked, "Do you want to take my Jeep?"

"Can we take the top down?" Mark asked.

"I haven't figured it out yet," Sienna replied. "It was hot today, so I left it up. But right now, the weather is perfect. Let's try!"

"I used to have a Jeep like this. We just need to pop out the two front panels." Mark had it done within two minutes. They put the panels in the back and were on their way.

Chapter 16

Everyone loved Palila's big heart, boisterous behavior and contagious laugh and were in awe of her surfing skills. Nobody could believe that, of all people, Palila had become so sick. The tall woman with high cheekbones, broad shoulders, long muscular legs and the honu tattoo on her upper arm had always been the picture of health. Everyone wanted to spend time with her before her soul passed from her diseased body and went to a better place.

Palila was expecting some friends this weekend but was content only seeing Nalu, Lani and her family. She was nervous about facing Mark and his new girlfriend Sienna. Even though she had been too proud to contact him, she had never stopped having feelings for Mark. And she wasn't sure who should watch over Nalu after she passed. Maybe it had been a mistake not accompanying him to the Keys back then. It had been terrible for Palila to never have a father, and now her daughter was growing up under the same circumstances. Her mother had always been overworked, doing hard manual labor from sunrise to sunset seven days a week, and Palila's life had basically been the same.

Palila had rested all day in anticipation of sitting on a

surfboard in the ocean this afternoon. The thought of it brought back thrilling memories of her surfing days. Her eyes sparkled with joyous tears.

She sat by the ocean behind Kōkī Beach House under a monkeypod tree. The big tree protected her from the sun's rays as she rested comfortably in a lawn chair, a thin colorful quilt spread across her legs and a pillow stuffed behind her back. The kids had all visited her and hung out down by the beach. They had swung on the old swing hanging from a big tree branch. Toys were still strewn all over the grass. Now they were all upstairs doing their homework, and Paolo was taking his afternoon nap. She looked across the ocean, listening to the water lapping against the lava rock and gazing at Alau Island in the distance. She remembered a time when she had camped illegally on Kōkī Beach with Mark, Josh and some others. They had been so young and carefree.

FLASHBACK

11 years ago @ Kōkī Beach

A young, vibrant Palila rode a big wave at Kōkī Beach. Everyone else had gotten pummeled by the fierce ocean and given up already. The group of friends sat underneath the trees lining the beach, drinking beer. They watched breathlessly as Palila tube rode inside the barrel of a breaking wave. She slowed down and purposely let herself drop off the board. Then she turned it around, got back on and paddled back out. She wasn't done yet.

"Brah, just like a pro." Josh jabbed Mark in the ribs with his elbow. "She's a daredevil, brah. Doesn't give up. And she's hot."

Mark looked out at the roaring ocean, not letting Palila out of his sight for a moment. He got up and walked over to the shoreline. He knew Palila was a strong surfer, but the wind had picked up, and the waves were unusually high. Mark wished she'd finish and come in. It was getting dark. The others sat by the campfire, playing ukulele, having another beer. He lost track of Palila out in the ocean. Josh walked up behind him.

Mark asked, "I can't see her anymore, can you?"

"No, but I'm sure she's fine. You just can't see her because she's not standing yet. She's way out there, just hanging on to her board. Watch the next wave, and you'll see her riding again."

They stood there for a while, watching and waiting. Nothing happened. There was still no sign of her. It was getting darker. They started panicking...

...when suddenly Palila dropped her surfboard in the sand behind them. She jumped in between the two men and took Mark into her arms, almost knocking him over. She had come out of the water behind the huli huli chicken truck. Palila laughed hysterically.

"I tricked the Grim Reaper again," she yelled. They chimed in with her contagious laughter.

****

BACK TO PRESENT TIME

Palila chuckled at her memory of happy days. But her smile

froze, and her eyes filled up with tears. This time she wasn't going to trick the Grim Reaper. *He is right there, out to get me,* she thought as a chill went down her spine.

Before she could get too sad, Nalu ran up. "Mom, we're all going down to the beach in fifteen minutes. Go put on your bathing suit and get ready!"

Palila turned toward Nalu. "Sure, Ku'uipo, my sweetheart."

She got up slowly and carefully. She knew it would take tremendous willpower to sit on that surfboard.

———————◦———————

The beach was crowded in the afternoon with guests shuttled from the local hotel and Road to Hāna tourists stopping for a quick visit and dip in the ocean. Max carefully led Palila into the water and helped her sit astride the surfboard as it swayed back and forth in the surf. This was no longer easy for Palila. Since her muscle mass had gone in her legs, she had a hard time keeping her balance. But she persevered. The water was so shallow that her toes touched the ground. Kai, Paolo and Nalu played around them in the shallow water. Lani, Luana and Paul watched from shore.

Palila had taken her scarf off. Despite her bald head and skin irritations from the medication, she was still beautiful. She held her head up proudly, ignoring the pitiful looks from the beach goers. Max held his arm around her waist as she sat on the surfboard.

"Can I come and sit with Mom?" Nalu asked Max. He looked at Palila who smiled and nodded. Nalu climbed up in front of her mother, assisted by Max. Palila held on to Nalu as Max pulled the surfboard through the knee-deep water along the shoreline. Kai and Paolo caught on and wanted to go for a ride as well. Lani got her surfboard at the back of the beach, leaning against the trees. She pushed it into the water and let Kai and Paolo climb up on the board. She caught up with Max, Palila and Nalu. They formed a little surf train and plowed through the water. Palila closed her eyes and leaned forward against Nalu. The warm salty water and soothing sound of the waves made everything better for a while.

A bit later, Palila rested under the shady trees on a comfortable bed that Lani had made for her out of some cozy blankets and pillows. Everyone else hung out in folding chairs and on towels, eating the delicious Thai food Paul and Luana had brought. Palila, exhausted from the unusual activity, had no appetite, but she was in her happy place surrounded by her favorite people. Lani sat down next to Palila and caressed her back.

"Mahalo for having us," said Palila. "You have no idea how great this feels after being cooped up in that moldy trailer for three months."

"I wish you'd come earlier," replied Lani. "You would've been welcome anytime."

They watched the kids run back down to the water.

"I never thought about having one of those bucket lists," said Palila. "But sitting on a surfboard again like today would have been on that list. It brought back all the memories of my fun surfing days. Oh, do I wish I could do that again, but I will soon, I guess. Maybe I'll come back as a honu, my favorite ocean creature," she said, smiling.

"I could see that happening." That thought made Lani smile as well. "Every time I see a honu, I'll think of you. We should tell Nalu the same thing. It will give her some comfort."

Lani leaned forward and gave her friend a gentle hug.

Chapter 17

The sun sat low as Sienna and Mark headed west on Honoapiilani Highway. The vast Pacific Ocean sparkled on the left, and the verdant West Maui Mountains on the right with the dark crevices between the ridges were stunning. Mark pointed at the island across the channel. "That's Lana'i over there. I wish we were more into whale season. We'd be seeing them breach and flap their tales and fins everywhere. There are only a few here this early."

"Oh, didn't I tell you I saw one this morning? I was sitting at the beach in Kihei having breakfast after picking up the Jeep, and a whale breached right in front of me!"

"Well, there you go. That's awesome!"

"When is whale season exactly?" asked Sienna.

"From December until April."

Sienna stared straight ahead at the road, nervously bouncing her knee. "I was thinking of taking the ferry to Lana'i tomorrow. Someone I talked to recommended it. And I want to go and see the Cat Sanctuary. Is it worth it?"

"Definitely. Just the ferry ride is worth it, and you'll probably see lots of spinner dolphins on the way. Lana'i is beautiful, very different than Maui. It has tall red cliffs. One of them is Puu Pehe, also called Sweetheart Rock. We'll have to google the story later. The beaches and reef are also beautiful. You can take the snorkel equipment I rented. You should go," he repeated. "I wish we could go together, but it doesn't look good this trip."

Sienna nodded. She might really go but didn't have to tell Mark she wasn't going by herself...

They drove through a shady stretch of road lined with large trees and entered the 300-foot Pali tunnel. When they came out of the tunnel, Sienna was blinded by the sun for a moment and put her sunglasses back on. A few minutes later they arrived in historic Lahaina, a busy little tourist town with shops, cafes and restaurants on both sides of the road. Tourists strolled up and down the sidewalks. The capitol of the Hawaiian Kingdom in the early 19th century, Lahaina also used to be a whaling village during the mid-1800s.

They passed a gigantic banyan tree on the ocean side, stretching over several blocks.

"We'll have to come here and hang out one evening. You'd probably like to go shopping," said Mark. "There's so much to see on Maui, I think you might have to extend your trip."

"I agree," she replied smiling.

Mark grinned at Sienna, reveling in his love for her. "Sienna, even though all this with Palila is going on, and I know it's really tough on you, I wanted to tell you I'm really happy you're here with me. I love you so much."

She put her hand on his.

"I'm sorry everyone has to go through this. I love you too, Mark."

136

Grateful for one another, they tried to shake off the sadness.

After passing through Front Street, they drove back onto the highway and headed toward the ritzy resorts and an upscale shopping mall in Kanaapali. Traffic was stop and go as they made their way past golf courses and beautiful hotels framed by the ocean behind them.

Mark pointed left. "Go into that parking garage. We're going to Black Rock first. There are usually some honu hanging out here, especially the most famous one on Maui named "Volkswagen". I'll ask around if anyone has seen him if we don't spot him. You can't miss him. He weighs about three hundred pounds."

They made their way along a walkway snaking against the ocean in front of the hotels, Kanaapali Beach Walk, and headed toward a big black rock, just as the name said.

"Black Rock, or the Rocky Point, was formed after one of the last lava flows on this side of Maui. The Hawaiian name for Black Rock is Pu'u Keka'a. Ancient Hawaiians called this the place their spirits jumped off to join their ancestors forever," Mark explained.

Teenagers hung out on top of the rock, cliff-jumping into the sparkling water and snorkeling around the lava rock. Mark and Sienna stepped onto the beach. It seemed too busy for honu to be hanging out. There were none on the shore, but Mark asked a few teenagers if they had seen honu in the water. They all reported seeing a really massive sea turtle swimming around.

"That was most likely Volkswagen," Mark said to Sienna and thanked the teenagers.

After a quick fifteen-minute drive on a curvy road heading west, they arrived at Honolua Bay.

They walked down a path leading through an enchanted forest with giant monkeypod trees full of vines, banyan trees with air roots, chickens roaming about and a little stream running along the path. The high canopy of thick trees blocked off the sun and it was a nice shady walk, until they stepped out into Honolua Bay. There were some honu hanging out on the left side and Mark spotted a couple of sea turtles in the water, but they were hawksbill sea turtles (honu'ea), the second most common sea turtle on Maui.

"This area doesn't seem affected, although I don't know how many sea turtles usually hang out here," said Mark.

Sienna didn't seem to hear him. She looked around, taking in all the beauty. "Wow, this is just amazing. We should come back and go snorkeling here." She pointed at all the people snorkeling in the water.

"We can do that on a weekday when I'm done working. Sorry that we're in such a rush today. We should get to Kapalua and Napili Bay, it's getting dark."

Sienna pointed to an island in the west across the water. "What's that? Molokai?"

Mark followed her gaze. "Yes, I think it is."

They made their way back to Kapalua Bay Beach and then finally Napili Bay. Several honu were hanging out for sunset on both beaches. Mark typed some notes for Josh into his phone. When Mark was done, he and Sienna stood at Napili Bay, arm in arm, watching the glowing sun dip into the ocean and turn the sky red to pink and purple.

"It feels like we haven't spent any time together yet," said Sienna. She looked up at him, and he pulled her close, bending down to press his lips to hers. Sienna wrapped her arms around Mark. They breathed each other in as they kissed. The sand warmed their bare feet. Sienna's dress billowed from the gentle breeze and tugged on her hair as they embraced each other.

There is never going to be a better moment to ask her, thought Mark. As they finally let go of each other, he pulled the ring box out of his pocket and got down on one knee. He opened the box, exposing the beautiful heirloom plumeria ring. Sienna gasped. Her hands flew to her mouth as she looked at the ring. She beamed, her eyes tearing as she stood there in the sunset.

"Sienna Brantley, I knew from the moment I met you that you were the one. You're smart, caring, witty and sexy as hell. I can't think of anyone else I want to spend the rest of my days and grow old with. I love you. Will you marry me?"

Sienna squealed, bouncing up and down as tears rolled down her face. "Yes, I will, Mark Baldwin."

He slipped the ring onto her finger. It fit perfectly. Mark stood, took her face in his hands and kissed her gently, then more passionately. He relished the feel of her against him, his heart filled to the brim with love for her. Sienna leaned into him, kissing him fervently. She never wanted this sensation to end.

When they finally pulled away from each other, they walked hand in hand over to the Sea House. The restaurant belonged to Napili Kai Resort on the west side of the beach. Not only did it have breathtaking ocean views, it was also well-known for its great food and live slack key guitar music.

Mark had reserved a table on the terrace. Torches lit up the perimeter, casting silhouettes of tall, swaying palm trees on both sides of the bay.

Just as the waiter walked up, a musician started playing soothing tropical rhythms.

"Aloha, guys, my name is Noa. Welcome to Sea House. I brought you some menus. We're still serving pau hana, happy hour, for another half hour and have some delicious pupus. Would you like that menu too?"

"Sounds good. Mahalo," said Mark.

"Do you want to take a look at the drink menu and put in an order, or shall I get you some water first and give you some time?"

Mark looked at Sienna and asked, "How about a mai tai?"

She looked down and stretched out her fingers to admire her new ring. "Sure. But only one. One of us needs to be the designated driver," she said, thinking of the previous day.

They turned toward the slack key guitar player, listening to the soulful Hawaiian music. The waiter brought them their drinks. It was the perfect atmosphere and they both refused to let the upcoming events ruin at least this one evening.

Chapter 18

It was still dark at Lahaina Harbor, but people were already boarding the ferry to Lana'i. Dawn was setting in, and it was promising to be a gorgeous day. Hundreds of tropical birds chirped in the giant banyan tree as Sienna rushed along the Pioneer Inn, trying to catch the ferry on time. She hadn't been able to find a parking space that she could stay in the entire day and was now running late. Tom stood at the ticket booth waiting for her. He didn't want to purchase a ticket for her before he knew she'd really show up.

"So glad to see you," he said as she rushed up.

"So sorry I'm late. I didn't think parking would be such an issue this early."

"I should have told you where to find long-term parking, I'm sorry." He turned around toward the ticket clerk and said, "Two roundtrips please, we'll take the five thirty ferry back."

Sienna got her wallet out and told the clerk she'd pay separately.

"Would you like to sit outside or inside?" asked Tom as they walked onto the ferry.

"Outside, of course." Sienna followed him up the stairs, and they sat down on a bench in the stern of the boat.

"I guess that was a dumb question on a beautiful day like today." He grinned and looked at her, his eyes sparkling.

Tension came up between them and she felt it necessary to clarify one thing.

"Tom, I really hope I'm not giving you a wrong impression. I want to make sure you know that I'm not interested in any type of flirt or relationship. I love Mark and really hope you and I can just be friends. Actually, he proposed to me last night. And I accepted."

He sat back, his eyes wide, then cleared his throat before saying, "Wow, congratulations." He wasn't ready for a new relationship after his wife's passing, but he certainly had been lonely. "Yes, of course. I'm glad you're coming along."

He held his hand up to shake hers. "Just friends. And no worries. I have female friends and it works. I also have four older sisters."

"Wow, that's a lot of estrogen to put up with."

She shook his hand, and they both smiled. Sienna really hoped it would work out that way. Four sisters meant he was used to being around a lot of women.

She sat back, relaxed and looked around as the boat departed. They drifted away from Lahaina Harbor and the Pioneer Inn as the sky lightened above the West Maui Mountains.

"So, what business takes you to Lana'i?" Sienna asked.

"It's crazy, but as you might know, you can close on a house via Zoom these days. My wife and I still owned property on Lana'i, and I just sold it to buy something bigger on Maui. We weren't able to take care of it properly or go often during the past few years, so it's been a rental and was becoming a bit of a money pit. I hired an old friend to empty and clean out the house and want to take one last look. We have another two weeks to get out."

"Won't that take you much longer than a quick visit?"

"No, don't worry, I've already been there for days and have taken all personal items out. I just want to take one last look and grab a photo album I forgot filled with dear memories. My friend Frank called me and wanted to ship it. But I thought I might as well go over and pick it up."

She nodded. It sounded like there were still some sentimental memories attaching him to the house.

"You can come if you want, but you can also go shopping. There are a few cute galleries and cafes in Lana'i City."

"We'll play it by ear. You might want to be by yourself with your memories," she replied. "Or maybe you could drop me off at the Cat Sanctuary and then go and take care of your house? I promised my girls I'd go and take a lot of pictures. We love cats. As a matter of fact, we own one of the Hemingway cats — or that's what we call him, he just happens to be polydactyl."

"Oh, that's cool. I've always wanted to go to the Cat Sanctuary. I'll come with you."

The ferry drove along the entire length of the island to reach the harbor. The prominent red lava cliffs of the island became visible as they approached Lana'i. Sienna leaned against the railing, watching the island pass by. A pod of glistening spinner dolphins jumped out of the water spinning around their own axis, just as the name suggested, and dove back in one by one. Sienna watched with her mouth gaping open. Tom stepped up next to her, smiling.

"Have you ever seen spinner dolphins this closely? They are amazing."

"No, I had never seen that species until during the hike at La Perouse," she replied. "I can't believe how fast they are."

"Did you bring snorkeling gear?" he asked. "We could go swimming to cool off in the afternoon."

"I brought my bathing suit, a towel, a pair of goggles and a snorkel." She pointed at her backpack. "The fins were too much to haul around all day. But that's fine, I'm a pretty good swimmer."

"Same here. Great minds think alike." He looked back out at the island.

She examined his hawk nose and protruding chin from the side. *What a great guy.* He noticed her gaze and opened his mouth to say something funny, diverting the awkward situation, but the captain announced their arrival at Lana'i Harbor.

The boat docked and the passengers disembarked. Tom's friend Frank had already parked a Jeep for them and left the key in a secret hiding place, so they didn't have to wait for a shuttle or take care of rental paperwork. They threw their backpacks into the back, climbed inside and were off to Lana'i City to have breakfast. Red dust whirled up behind them as they drove up a winding road, leaving the ocean behind.

Pointing at the big pine trees lining the road, Tom explained, "These are Cook Island pines that were planted because there's such little rain on the island. Pine needles extract moisture from the atmosphere. They can take in up to

200 gallons of water per day and somehow the scientists have figured out how to catch that water."

"Wow, I've never heard of that," she said. The landscape didn't even look Hawaiian to her. It was all volcanic scrubland but not as lush and tropical as Maui. Driving into Lana'i City was like going back in time.

"This was all originally built for the workers of Dole's pineapple plantation in the 1920s," explained Tom.

Simple houses with small yards rowed up along the red dirt road. The pines were everywhere here too. Tom steered the Jeep onto a small side road and stopped in front of a quaint white cottage with blue doors and accents. The sign said: *Blue Ginger Café*. They went inside to order, filled their cups with fresh Hawaiian coffee from a giant thermos and came back out to sit at the terrace's outdoor seating.

"So, where's your house?" asked Sienna.

"You can walk from here." He pointed down the road. "Just down this way. I can go and take care of that first while we're here, if that's okay with you."

"Of course. How about I walk over there with you, and then I can walk around and explore for a bit while you look through your things one more time."

"Perfect."

A young girl came out with two plates piled high with giant breakfast burritos and fruit. They ate with gusto.

Sienna talked to him like a long-lost brother.

"So, your wife died of cancer?"

"Yes, ovarian cancer. We thought she was in complete remission after five years, and then, another year later, *bam*. It was back and had spread everywhere with a vengeance. There was nothing we could do anymore."

"What a weird coincidence. We were obviously meant to meet. Same last name. Same profession. Mark lived here for a year after college. He ran into his old girlfriend from back then, and she's dying of ovarian cancer. She has a few more days or a week to live at the most."

Tom looked at Sienna and reached out to touch her shoulder. Memories about the last weeks and days with his wife flooded back. "I'm so sorry to hear that. It was a terrible, painful death for my wife."

"That's why I came here with you to spend the day. I don't know how to handle the situation. I'm really enjoying one day of distraction before we go to Hāna to see her tomorrow. Oh, and she has a daughter which is obviously his. He had no idea about her."

"Wow." He paused for a second to digest that information. "So, are you guys going to adopt the daughter and take her back to Florida with you?"

"I have no idea. The ex-girlfriend broke up with Mark because she didn't want to move away from Maui. Ever. So, she might not want her daughter to leave either. I think she was planning on the daughter growing up with some good friends. I don't even know if there's enough time to settle things. I also don't know if Mark still has feelings for her. He's very upset about the whole situation and not himself right now."

"You must be very upset too. I guess this isn't how you were expecting to spend your vacation."

"No, but that's not important considering the overall

situation." She looked down as her eyes filled with tears again. "Our breakfast is getting cold. Let's talk about something happier. Tell me about your daughters."

"Oh, they're a hoot. They're beautiful, but they get in trouble all the time. They mess with their boyfriends by pretending to be each other. I could tell you stories about them all day."

They sat there chatting and enjoying their breakfast until they were too stuffed to eat one more forkful.

Chapter 19

As the sun rose above Olowalu Beach and Camp Olowalu, an old rugged fisherman shuffled down to the water. He carried a fishing rod, a stack of buckets and a small three-legged folding chair under his arm. At the water's edge, he set up his chair and preparing his fishing rod. He scanned the beach for honu. A few hung out on the east side in the sand. A peaceful morning.

Two younger fishermen wearing baseball caps and dark hoodies snuck around underneath the trees lining the beach. They didn't seem happy to see him. They signaled to each other and walked over to the fisherman.

He looked up from trying to pierce some squid onto the hook.

"Hey brahs, howzit going?"

"Great. And yourself? You fish here often?"

"Used to. But work kept me from coming lately. I'm retired now and hope to pick it back up. Live right down the road."

"Well, we wish you a good haul." They strolled down the beach with their hands in their pockets toward the honu but curved around them, keeping an appropriate distance.

The first fisherman pretended to be busy with his fishing

rod and watched them walk away out of the corner of his eye. He stood up, cast his rod and then sat back down.

The two young men turned around inconspicuously, heading back toward the fisherman, then made a beeline to the trees. One of them typed into his phone, *Abort. Someone's here.*

As soon as the two men were out of sight, Charlie fished a walkie-talkie out of one of the buckets. "Charlie for Neill."

Another undercover officer sitting in the parking lot in a beaten-up old Ford Fiesta picked up his walkie. "Go for Neill, Charlie."

"They're coming up to the parking lot now. No action required, but make sure you get their license plate."

The two young men didn't get into a car but kept walking all the way to the camping area and crawled into one of the smaller tents.

"They're camping here," said Neill.

"Get their campsite number," Charlie instructed him. "We can get their info from their reservation."

Neill got out of his car and started walking toward the campsite.

Sienna and Tom finished their breakfast and drove to the road's dead end. Tom stopped at the last residence, a yellow cottage surrounded by tall pine trees. Traces of a tropical garden remained, but over the years it had turned into an overgrown jungle.

"Would you like to come in and take a look?" asked Tom.

"Sure." Sienna was curious. The picturesque cottage

needed a new coat of paint and the rocking chairs on the front porch had splintered apart.

As they walked up to the front door, Tom warned Sienna. "Be careful not to step on this one plank, it's a bit brittle."

Crack. Sienna stepped onto the plank just as he warned her. Tom jumped back, pulling her arm so she didn't fall. But everything was fine. They both laughed.

"Well, as you can see, we sold the cottage 'as is.'"

"It's charming," Sienna replied.

They stepped inside a living room with old wood floors and a view into the jungle-like side yard. It was already emptied except for an old couch and sideboard.

"What a shame that you have to sell it, but I can see it would be hard always taking the ferry to get here."

"We used to come here on vacation with the girls a lot, but I haven't worked much since my wife passed away. I really need the money for a place in Kihei. You might have seen the prices there." He rolled his eyes.

He looked through the sideboard and found the photo album his friend Frank had told him about. Lost in his thoughts, he flipped through the pages.

"I'm going give you some privacy and walk over to the hotel and tour the gardens. Could you pick me up there when you're done?"

"Yes, perfect," he said without looking up.

Sienna left the cottage and walked down the road leading to the five-star hotel in Lana'i City. There seemed to be two parts of this hotel, one in town and one beachfront property down by Hulopoe Beach and Pu'u Pehe. The resort in town boasted a botanical garden with lots of indigenous plants.

Sienna walked through the Japanese-inspired lobby and into the tropical garden. Tall palm trees swayed. She walked down a path, relaxed by the mere surroundings. It seemed like she was the only person here. As she sat by a koi pond, an older woman carrying a basket full of flowers walked up and said "Aloha" as she handed Sienna a white blossom.

"Mahalo," said Sienna as she looked at the unique flower. "This is beautiful. Can you tell me what it is?"

The woman smiled and replied, "This is a Naupaka flower. It's a common beach and mountain shrub. Can you see how the bloom looks like it's just half of a flower? According to an old legend, an ancient Hawaiian Princess, Naupaka, fell in love with a commoner named Kaui. Her parents wouldn't let her marry him. They were desperate and went to get advice from a kahuna in the mountains. He advised them to pray at a temple, but no answers were sent. Princess Naupaka tore the flower she had been wearing in her hair into two pieces and gave half of it to Kaui. She told him to live by the sea while she'd stay in the mountains. They separated with broken hearts. When the plants saw this, they started blooming with only half a flower."

"What a nice legend," said Sienna. "Mahalo for sharing it with me."

"We do a garden tour every evening and talk about the myths and legends of the local plants and flowers. I hope to see you there."

Sienna regretted that she couldn't stay longer but enjoyed the moment and continued walking through the beautiful gardens. Her phone beeped with a text message from Tom. He was at the hotel to pick her up. She walked out front and climbed into the Jeep.

"Did you find anything else in the house?"

"No, not really anything with a sentimental value like the photo album," he replied, "but I'm very glad I was able to go and say goodbye to that old place. Lots of memories there."

Sienna nodded. She was happy he'd been able to go one more time.

"So, now it's your turn for some sightseeing. We're on our way to Shipwreck Beach. Have you heard of it?"

"No, I haven't. Sounds like something out of a pirate movie."

"How about you let me surprise you, and you'll see when we get there?"

They drove through the barren countryside behind the hotel to the opposite side of the island from the harbor. After taking a left onto a dirt road, Tom put the Jeep into four-wheel drive so they wouldn't get stuck. He drove down the sandy path until it ended with the sign: *Shipwreck Beach.* They walked along the beach and climbed over lava rock to see the giant rusty hull of the World War II Ship. It sat in the shallow water, purposely sunk as an economic means of disposal.

Tom bent down, picked up a beautiful shell and handed it to Sienna. She thanked him and asked, "Wouldn't this be a nice place to go swimming? It's getting a little hot."

"Unfortunately, it's not. The winds in this channel between Lana'i and Molokai create strong currents. That's why it's called Shipwreck Beach. Many ships have sunk here."

Sienna's hair blew in the wind. Its color matched the rusty

ship.

"Let me take some pictures of you," he said and snapped a few shots with his phone. He studied her and the background. "Look out at the ocean." *Click.* He had a good eye for composition and lighting and proudly showed her one of the photos, standing close as he swiped through his camera roll. Heat rolled off them and the soft hairs on his arm tickled Sienna. She stepped aside, uncomfortable with how attracted she felt to him. Here she was, newly engaged, feeling this tension with another man the next day. Tom noticed her discomfort and backed off.

Sienna tried to casually continue the conversation. "Wow, that looks cool. You're a good photographer. Could you please send those to me?"

He nodded and said, "Now, let's take a selfie." He turned around, strategically positioning himself next to her, but at a safe distance, stretched his arm out and took a few photos of them with the ship and Molokai in the background "Now let's look for the hiking trail leading to the petroglyphs. They're very cool."

They walked back toward the Jeep, then Tom led Sienna up a hill leading away from the beach, past some stone alignments of ancient house sites and through fields of lava rock. The sun beat down on them. Sienna felt her jet lag kicking in again, but she enjoyed the great views. He led her up to a pile of boulders and pointed at some ancient rock carvings. "I've read that this is probably a hunting scene with men, a horse, a dog and either a pig or cow."

"Do you have any idea how old they are?"

"I don't. I read on one website that they're about two hundred years old, but I don't know if that's correct."

"I hate to sound dumb, but what's the difference between petroglyphs and hieroglyphs? I've never heard of petroglyphs."

He grinned. "There is no dumb question. I had to look it up myself the first time I heard of this. Petroglyph is a rock carving and hieroglyph is an element of an ideographic writing system."

"That makes sense."

He looked at his watch. "Okay, our time on Lana'i is limited, so we should go to the Cat Sanctuary next. We can stop in Lana'i City on the way through and grab some sandwiches. There's no place to buy lunch around the Cat Sanctuary and Pu'u Pehe."

"Sounds good." She was glad to have her own personal tour guide.

They headed to the southwestern side of the island. After making a generous donation, they got cat treats from a friendly employee. "Lana'i Cat Sanctuary is home to over six hundred feral and abandoned cats," she explained. "They're also called Lana'i Lions and many are up for adoption."

Sienna and Tom walked into the first fenced-in area. Sienna sat down at a picnic table. Cats in all shapes, sizes and colors jumped up begging for treats. Tom took countless pictures of her: Sienna looking adoringly at a cat she was petting, *click*. Sienna turning her head, *click*. Her hair blowing in the breeze, *click*. Her head cocked at a different angle, searching out other cats, *click*. Sienna laughing at a silly cat's antics, *click*.

"Do you know that by starting this sanctuary, not only the cats but also many of the island's endangered birds were saved too?" asked Tom. Sienna nodded. Another *click*. That made absolute sense. She looked at her watch.

"It's about six p.m. in Florida. Do you mind if I try facetiming with Leo and the girls?"

"No, of course not," replied Tom. "Go ahead."

Tom hesitated. He wasn't sure if Sienna's family in Florida was supposed to see him. "I'll go look at the senior cats in the meantime."

She smiled. It might bring up strange questions about why she was with someone other than Mark, and she wondered again if she was doing the right thing and not getting herself into trouble. But nothing was happening. She and Tom were just friends.

Lindsey was the older of the two sisters, so Sienna dialed her number.

"Hey, Aunt Sienna! We're just having dinner with grandma and grandpa!"

"Hey, Lindsey, hi everyone!" Lindsey turned her phone and moved it around the table so Sienna could see everyone. Sydney was there, but Leo was out with his girlfriend.

"Hey, Sydney, hey, Lilly, hey, Grandma and Grandpa!"

Everyone looked up from their plates, waving and smiling.

"Look where I am." Sienna panned the phone across a group of cats.

"Oh, we're so jealous!" said Lindsey, Lilly and Sydney. "Can we come next time? We wanna come and visit those cats!"

"Yes, we'll have to plan a vacation here. I need to show you everything. It's so beautiful here."

Sydney asked, "Is my dad there too?"

"No, he's working right now. I came here by myself for the day. I'll see him tonight and say hi to him from you, okay?"

Sienna talked to the kids' grandparents, Richard and Rose, a little while longer to check if everything was okay with Leo and everyone's schools, and then she ended the call. She stared into the distance, amazed at how much she missed this bunch that she had barely known a year ago. She followed Tom into the senior cat section. He was sitting on a chair surrounded by five cats. Two were in his lap.

"Wow, they really seem to like you," she said laughing.

"Yeah, older women have always had a thing for me," he replied.

He stood up, brushing the cat hair off his pants. "We should go. We have about two hours to hike up to Pu'u Pehe and go swimming. Then we need to catch the ferry."

———————◦———————

Pu'u Pehe, also known as Sweetheart Rock, was a triangular sea stack 150 feet off the peninsula separating Manele Bay from Hulopoe Bay. Tom and Sienna parked the car and hiked past the beach up to the imposing red cliffs.

"The legend says a Maui princess was kidnapped by a young Lana'i warrior. She was so beautiful that he didn't want other men to see her and put her in a sea cave near the rock. During a storm, the tide rose, and the princess drowned in the cave. Heartbroken, he buried her in a tomb on top of the rock and then jumped to his death."

"What a sad story," said Sienna. She stared down at Pu'u Pehe, distracted and still thinking of her kids in the Keys.

"How are the kids?" asked Tom.

"It's the first time I've been separated from them. They're handling it well, though. They have each other, and their grandparents dote on them."

"That's nice. My girls' grandparents were in the Hudson Valley. It was always tough to be so far away. Especially when they became too frail to travel."

"How about their mom's side of the family? Are they still around?"

"Yes, they live in Hāna. We spent a lot of time there when the girls were smaller. It's a very traditional old Hawaiian family. It took them a long time to accept that their daughter was married to a haole, a white guy. But now they love me."

He looked her straight in the eyes and grinned like a mischievous little boy.

What's not to love? she thought.

They made their way back to the beach and had a picnic under the shady monkeypod trees. Sienna automatically scanned the beach for honu. "Are there a lot of honu in Lana'i?"

"I've seen some here. I'm not sure if they're as frequent as on Maui, but they are certainly around here too, especially in Manele Bay and here at Hulopoe Beach Park."

"You know, Mark and his colleagues are having an issue right now with honu disappearing from the beaches. They think there might even be poachers attempting to steal them. Did you hear about billionaire Julian Jensen bragging about being able to buy one on TV?"

"Yes, I happened to have the news on that morning. The locals must not like him very much right now..."

Sienna nodded. Tom stood up.

"Speaking of honu. Let's go swimming and see if we can spot any. I'm ready to cool off." He pointed at a building behind the trees. "We can change over there in the restrooms."

Sienna was ready as well. The ocean looked cool and refreshing. She grabbed her bathing suit, walked over to the bathrooms and they were both in the water in no time. Several honu swam around them in the crystal-clear water. Mesmerized, Sienna held her breath and watched the beautiful creatures. Further out, they found an abundance of marine reef life. Sienna frolicked in the water. She hadn't been this carefree in a while.

Much too soon, they were back on the ferry, but it had been a long day and they were tired. Sienna received a text message from Mark.

Shall I meet you in Lahaina, and we'll have dinner there?

Sienna didn't want to chance Mark waiting for her at the ferry in Lahaina and catching her hanging out with Tom.

She replied, *How about Café Olé in Kihei instead? I'd rather save Lahaina for a night when we can stay longer and shop for a while. Really tired, and don't we have to get up early tomorrow? Meet you there at 7?*

He replied, *Sure. See you then. Great place.*

The ferry ride was smoother than Sienna expected. Everyone said it could get quite rocky on the way back to Maui, and Sienna had prepared herself by buying a ginger-based nausea relief shot, available in most Maui stores, called Hana

Tonic.

She and Tom talked more about the kids, his daughters and his wife's death. He talked about hospice and choked up a bit telling Sienna how quickly his wife had passed once she left hospice and came home. Her family's Hawaiian beliefs had helped them immensely.

"Most souls proceed to the afterlife or underworld," he explained. "The afterlife is described as similar to life on earth. A soul with exceptional spiritual power, mana, could become an 'aumakua, ancestral guardian spirit. Honu are believed to be 'aumakua. That's why Hawaiians consider them to be spiritual and very special. There are also lapu, wandering ghosts that remain among the living, but they're generally regarded as harmful and avoided. These wandering ghosts are called 'Night Marchers.'"

Sienna liked hearing about these beliefs. Palila might have the same ones. Though she realized she could talk to Tom about anything, she tried to remain friendly yet distant.

The ferry approached Lahaina Harbor. The sun was just setting, and the sky and the West Maui Mountains blazed with every color of the rainbow.

"Thank you very much for the great day. I really enjoyed spending time with you," said Tom as they said goodbye. "Stay in touch."

Sienna gave him a long friendly hug. "You have no idea how nice it was to just relax, see something new and have some good conversations. I needed that distraction. Thank you. And good luck with your new job."

They went their separate ways.

Chapter 20

The next morning, Mark and Sienna departed for their two-night stay in Hāna. They packed a few changes of clothes in two duffel bags and took Sienna's Jeep. They were subdued but tried not to let the reason for their trip get them down too much.

Mark started a casual conversation by talking about work. "We were very short-staffed yesterday. Nora called off and a few volunteers didn't show up."

Sienna just nodded.

"So, tell me about Lana'i," said Mark.

"It was amazing. We need to take the kids to the Cat Sanctuary one day, and Shipwreck Beach was awesome too. We even saw some ancient Petroglyphs."

"We? I thought you went by yourself?"

"Well, I wasn't the only one there," she said quickly, breaking out in a sweat. One lie always led to others...

They passed the old Puunene Sugar Mill with its tall smokestack and the Sugar Museum on Hansen Road and soon arrived in Pai'a. Even though it looked tempting, they didn't stop. They weren't tourists today and were anxious to get to Hāna.

"We could stop here for dinner on the way back on Sunday," said Mark as he noticed Sienna looking longingly out the window at the fun shops and galleries.

She smiled. "Sure."

After they passed Pai'a, Mark took a left into Ho'okipa Beach Park since Sienna hadn't been here yet. She had to see the place with the most honu on Maui. They walked past some fruit and jewelry vendors up to the observation point railing. Wind surfers fought the waves, holding onto their colorful sails and performing amazing stunts. Sienna held her breath as a surfer got pummeled by the waves.

Mark laughed, feeling sorry for the surfer, but he told Sienna, "I used to be that guy. I never really got the hang for surfing even though I tried for hours and hours. Then I met Palila who was really accomplished, and she taught me—"

He hesitated. He didn't know if it was okay to talk about these memories, but it didn't seem to bother Sienna. They had talked about Mark's ex-wife and Sienna's ex-husband, and this was nothing different. She was glad he was opening up to her and replied matter-of-factly. "I can't imagine you not being able to surf, you're so athletic."

"Well, maybe since I'm so tall, I wasn't very coordinated when it came to getting up at the right time. I finally got the hang of it though. If you're interested, you should give it a try at Hāmoa Beach. I think Max, Lani's husband, is quite a good surfer."

"Uh huh," she responded absently. She was busy wrapping the hair blowing in her face into a ponytail.

"Let me help you." Mark lovingly pulled her hair back. She

adored his nurturing manner and gave him a quick hug. He pulled her closer and kissed her.

A lady asked, "Are you folks honeymooners?"

They let go of each other and smiled. "No, but we just got engaged." Mark was so glad he had found the right opportunity to propose to Sienna.

He pointed down at the beach. "Look at all the honu down there. It's a lot but still only half as many as usual. Do you want to go down and see them?"

"Sure," she replied, and they walked down the path leading to the beach. The waves were so strong that the spray felt like a gentle rain. The honu rested in the sand in a roped-off area to the right. Tourists stood there taking pictures, and everything made a peaceful impression.

Once they were back at the Jeep, the wind died down a little. They took the two front panels off, and Sienna tied a flowery scarf around her head. They followed the winding road. It narrowed the deeper they drove into the rainforest. Lush bamboo canes hung into the road, creating a shady canopy. Steep hills led up into the mountains to the right. Water trickled down the rocks, leaving moisture and humidity. The abyss leading to the ocean lay steep below them to their left. They could almost touch the crowns of the African tulip trees with their bright red blooms that literally looked like giant tulips. The hills and lush rainforest were something they didn't have in Florida, and Sienna truly enjoyed the drive.

They passed a stand of rainbow eucalyptus trees that looked like their trunks had been colored with crayons. After the Garden of Eden, some great waterfalls, and narrow bridges in hairpin curves, they arrived at the Ke'anae Peninsula. It was an area full of history with an old Hawaiian village, a church, some of the island's only remaining taro fields and amazing views of the Hāna coast.

Mark took a left and drove down a bumpy paved road leading down to the peninsula. He stopped at the famous banana bread stand and bought a few loaves for Lani's family. Then they continued to an older house a few hundred yards down the road.

Auntie Charlene was waiting for Mark and Sienna to pick up a new batch of herbs she had harvested for Ana. Everyone passing through who knew Palila picked up herbs and brought them to Ana. There weren't enough in her own little garden. Auntie Charlene also gave them more ginger candy and a big box with other fruits and vegetables.

"Mahalo for stopping by guys. Please tell Palila I'll be there on Sunday. I want to see her and that brave daughter of hers."

They drove all the way down to the other side of the peninsula and looked out at the beautiful coastline. Strong waves pounded against the lava rock. Moku Mana Islet Seabird Sanctuary sat in the distance looking like it had broken off the main part of the island. A lonely little pony stood behind a fence, begging for pets with its big brown eyes. The old stone church surrounded by tall coconut palm trees, Ke'anae Congregational Church, was the perfect photo opportunity. Mark moved next to Sienna, and she took a selfie.

"Show me your photos from yesterday," said Mark.

"Let's do that later," she replied quickly. She might have some photos with Tom on her camera roll. "It's too bright out here."

"Okay, let's get to Coconut Glen's next," he replied and gave her a kiss. "I'm craving ice cream."

"When are we supposed to be in Hāna?" asked Sienna.

"Not until this afternoon. Palila usually has a massage by Ana the healer or meditates in the morning, and then she sleeps for a while. Lani said she gets very tired. So, I can visit for a bit this afternoon, and I'll ask her when she wants to meet you."

"Okay," replied Sienna, bracing herself for a sad few days.

After driving a few more miles, they arrived at Coconut Glen's famous stand with the vegan ice cream. Glen, a good friend of Lani's family, offered to assist with anything Palila needed. Everyone in the community knew and cared about Palila and wanted to help. That was true mālama, which meant to give back, take care of yourself, others and the land, the 'āina.

They passed a sign stating they had arrived in Hāna, "The land of the low laying clouds, Ka'Āina o Ka Lani Ha'aha'a." Sienna, excited to finally be in Hāna, looked over at Mark. He stared out at the road, in a different world, looking troubled and lost. Sienna put her hand on his arm. "Mark, if you ever want to talk, please let me know. I'm here for you."

He inhaled and shifted in his seat, waking up from his trance and shaking the sadness off, but he obviously didn't want to talk about it. Sienna felt excluded and wished he would talk to her.

Trying to be more upbeat for Sienna and change the subject, Mark said, "It doesn't look like much changed here in the last ten years." They came up to a Blue Tropics Orchids sign on the side of the road, pointing to the right. Mark slowed and turned down the small bumpy road. Sienna wondered where he was going.

"We need to stop by Lani and Luana's nursery and get the keys. I told you we're staying in Luana and Paul's house, didn't I?"

"You mentioned they weren't sure if we could stay in a cottage across from Waioka Pond or in their house."

"Yeah, turns out the cottage is rented this weekend, so we're staying in their house. It's probably better because it's closer to Lani's house and Hāmoa Beach, even though we might have less privacy."

Mark continued down the road lined with little cottages on both sides until they arrived at a big greenhouse adorned with a tropical mural on the front wall. Chickens roamed the sandy parking lot, picking the sand for something edible. A proud peacock marched along, refusing to get out of the Jeep's way. It was idyllic. Finally, the peacock strolled to the side. Mark parked next to an old SUV, and they got out and walked inside.

Nobody was in the greenhouse. Mark and Sienna walked to the front to see if there was an office they had overlooked. There was indeed an office, but the door was closed, and nobody was inside. They walked deeper into the greenhouse and this time kept walking all the way to the back, where they finally discovered Lani and Luana. They looked like two beautiful Hawaiian sisters standing at a large potting bench full of bark, potting orchids in assembly line fashion and fully immersed in what they were doing.

"Aloha, ladies?" Mark felt bad taking them away from what they were doing.

They looked up simultaneously.

"Are you Lani and Luana? I'm Mark Baldwin, Palila's friend, and this is Sienna Brantley."

They put their pots and plants down, came around the table and shook Mark and Sienna's hands.

"Aloha, we're so glad you could make it," said Lani.

"We're so glad we could come too, and thanks for letting us stay at your house. It's very generous of you." He looked at Lani, then her mother as he asked,

"Lani, I assume? And Luana?"

They nodded.

"This is Sienna, my girlfriend. It's so nice to meet you. How is Palila doing? And Nalu?"

"Palila is getting very weak, but she's calm and in good spirits. Ana, our elder, is meditating a lot with her. Nalu is okay. She has her sad moments, but our kids are distracting her pretty good," replied Lani.

"Let me get the keys," said Luana as she headed toward the front office. "Please follow me."

"Your nursery is beautiful," said Sienna, following Luana through the rows of orchids and other tropicals.

"Mahalo, it's our passion."

"I can tell."

Luana handed Sienna a set of keys and explained, "This big key is for the entrance on the right side of the house. You have your own bathroom and little kitchen. It's like a mother-in-law suite."

"That's great. That way we won't feel like we're getting on your nerves," Mark said smiling.

"We're planning on having dinner around six thirty at our house. Can you join us?" asked Lani. "We're not sure if Palila will make it, she doesn't have much of an appetite anymore and can't sit very long, but Nalu has been eating with us."

"We'd love to," they said. Mark and Sienna turned to leave the greenhouse.

"Oh, hang on a second guys," said Luana. She grabbed a few stems of pink ginger, a protea, a heliconia bloom and some decorative leaves and put together the most wonderful exotic flower arrangement in just a few minutes. It was not only her passion, but a skill she had been practicing for over thirty years now, and it showed.

She handed the arrangement to Sienna with a smile and won another friend for life.

Chapter 21

Josh received an emergency call from the Maui Turtle Rescue. A call had come in about an injured honu at Makena Cove, less than ten minutes from the house.

"I'm on my way," he said. He was hoping to meet Nora there. She had to stop at the Turtle Rescue on her way and get the van with some emergency supplies: betadine, scissors, cotton swabs, baby wipes.

Josh arrived at the pretty bay surrounded by single family homes and tall palm trees. He walked along the water and then climbed through some dry shrubs to a secluded beach where the honu usually hung out. Neither the injured honu nor any other ones lay on the beach. He walked along the water to see if the honu had gone back in and was floating somewhere, but he couldn't see any. There were usually a few here this early in the morning. He went back to his car for his coffee and sat down at a picnic table, drinking a few sips as he looked out at the ocean and watched night turn into day.

His mobile phone rang, and he answered. Nora sounded upset, as if she were crying.

"Josh, I just got here. The outside door was open and the door to your office too. Someone made a huge mess looking for something, and some of the equipment is missing."

"Stay right where you are, I'm going to call my contact with the Wailuku Police Department. Don't touch anything for now."

He looked out at the ocean one more time and cursed, then dialed O'Shen's number.

O'Shen answered right away. She was on her way to her office.

"Aloha, O'Shen. My intern just called. There was a burglary at our offices. I told her to wait and not touch anything. Can you send someone over?"

O'Shen took an immediate left at the next side road and performed a risky U-turn in the fast-moving traffic. The approaching cars slowed down and honked. O'Shen didn't even pay attention and continued back in the direction she had just come from. She sped but didn't turn her sirens on. She called her colleague, Officer Christine Kalua, to meet her at Maui Turtle Rescue as soon as possible.

"Hey, Christine, we have a break-in at Maui Turtle Rescue. Can you meet me there ASAP?"

"Sure," replied Christine who was already in the office, getting ready for a boring day. She turned off her computer and jumped up.

O'Shen and Josh arrived at Maui Turtle Rescue at the same time. They walked up to Nora who sat on a chair in front of the door being comforted by some of her girlfriends who worked in the shops in the same plaza.

"We'll have forensics come in and sweep the place for fingerprints," said O'Shen. "Have you already checked whether something important is missing?" she asked Nora.

"I saw that one of our big jugs of betadine is missing. That's not expensive but hard to get here, so whoever did this might have a sick honu that needs treatment." She thought for a second. "One of the tools is missing that we use to remove the tracking devices from the honus' carapaces. But it could've just fallen onto the floor. It's such a mess in there…"

"It would make sense that they want to remove the trackers if they have any honu," said Josh.

"Besides that, I haven't looked around anymore. I really didn't want to go in there and touch things. Josh told me not to." She looked at him, her big blue eyes filling up with tears again.

The forensics colleagues arrived and disappeared into Josh's office with their equipment.

O'Shen and Christine examined the locks that had been easily broken. They started questioning some of the employees from the shops in the plaza who walked past the Maui Turtle Rescue on their way to and from work. Nobody had seen anything suspicious though. The intruders must have been here before regular business hours.

"So, another thing I wanted to mention," said Josh to O'Shen, "is that I was called for a honu emergency. When I showed up at the site, there were no honu around. I wonder if they were trying to keep us away from the office. Although, there's really nothing valuable to steal here except the honu." He hesitated and turned around toward Nora. "Have you checked on all our honu yet? Are any of them missing?"

She jumped up, her eyes popping open, and ran over to the

basins in the courtyard to count them. Then she walked outside to a bigger basin and counted again. None of the honu were missing.

The forensics guys came back out. "We found quite a few fingerprints but of course they could also be from the employees. We'll have to check if we find any of them in the system."

"Thanks, guys," said O'Shen. Then she turned toward Josh. "Well, there's nothing more we can do right now other than keep up with the surveillance and maybe add someone to watch this area."

"Mahalo," said Josh. He got ready to go back home. Today was his day off. He looked at Nora who could go back home too, but still looked very upset after what had happened.

"How about a coffee at the general store after this scare before we head into our weekend?" he asked, feeling a bit sorry for her.

"Sure," she replied smiling. They walked over to the general store, grabbed two cups of coffee and sat out front at one of the tables.

As they sat in the morning sun drinking their coffee and chatting, Nora looked at Josh and decided to tell him something she had been worrying about.

"Josh, I need to tell you something..."

"What is it?" he replied.

"This really nice guy has been hitting on me..."

Josh looked at her quizzically. Why would she be telling him personal things like that?

"He seems perfect. Handsome, two years older than me,

drives a nice car, has been taking me out to nice dinners... But it seems too good to be true. I can't get rid of the feeling that he's just going out with me to get information about what we do here at the turtle rescue. He said he works as the personal assistant of this wealthy guy on Lanai and keeps asking me the strangest questions. Like yesterday he asked me when we all start working and then today the break in... And he's been asking me about meds for honu and I told him about betadine... So, now that the betadine's missing, that really makes me wonder..."

Josh listened up. "Do you mean he works for Julian Jensen?"

Nora nodded.

"Do you mind if I call O'Shen and put her on speakerphone? That does sound quite suspicious..."

She nodded again. Josh picked up his mobile phone, dialed O'Shen's number.

"Hey, O'Shen. Nora and I are still here at the harbor and Nora brought something to my attention. Could we please have a word with you?"

"I'm still here in Ma'alaea Harbor too. I've been sitting in my car, stuck on a conference call. I'll be right over," she said. "That's easier than talking on the phone."

Two minutes later, O'Shen walked up to the general store. She looked at Josh and Nora and asked in her usual brisk manner, "Do you guys want anything?" as she walked into the store without even stopping. They just shook their heads. A few minutes later, O'Shen stepped out with a cup of black coffee and sat down.

"Sorry about that, I really need a coffee." She looked at them. "So what's going on?"

"Why don't you do most of the talking?" said Josh, looking at Nora.

Nora nodded and looked at O'Shen. "As I just told Josh, I met this guy, Julian Jensen's assistant, who I think is taking advantage of me and trying to get information about honu. His name is Ryan. He had just asked me yesterday when I'm working today, and now the break in right before I arrived..."

O'Shen digested and thought for a while, then she had an idea. "Maybe we should turn things around and WE take advantage of him... You pretend you don't suspect anything and keep giving him the info he wants or give him wrong info. Maybe at some point we can set a trap for him."

Josh was worried about Nora. "Won't that bring Nora in danger?"

"We'll keep them under surveillance every time they get together. Also, if okay with you, Nora, we'll monitor your phone. Do you ever talk to him or do you guys just text like most of us nowadays?"

"Yeah, we text mostly."

"That's even better," said O'Shen. "That way we have everything in writing." She got up. "Okay, guys, sorry, I have to leave, I have an appointment. But thanks for your cooperation, Nora, and I promise you'll be safe. It doesn't seem that this guy is out to harm you. He just obviously wants a honu... I'll be in touch."

She exchanged phone numbers with Nora and walked away. Josh and Nora looked at their phones. They were both shocked about how late it was. Josh had to pick up the kids, and Nora had plans as well.

"Well, thanks for coming out with this, Nora. I really appreciate your honesty."

"Of course," she replied, and they both went about their day. Josh had a bit more respect for her after this incident, and Nora was a bit more professional and a bit less flirtatious.

———————◦◦◦———————

Josh picked up his kids, Alana and Kimo, from the pretty cottage in North Kihei that he and Melanie had bought before they had kids. They had bought the fixer upper for a great price and had still barely been able to afford it. It hurt Josh every time he saw the cottage surrounded by lush hibiscus, plumerias and tall palm trees. He had renovated it for months and put so much blood, sweat and tears into it. They had a few very happy years and made so many memories.

It was tough dealing with his ex-wife. She blamed him for the breakup because he hadn't been able to forgive her. Even though she didn't want him to see the kids because she wanted to end the "Josh chapter," she had to realize how happy they were to see their dad.

The kids ran out the front door and hugged him, screaming, "Daddy, Daddy, Daddy!" Melanie's new boyfriend Nick, an athletic guy in his late thirties, puttered around in the background, making breakfast. *He's probably happy to have a weekend without the kids,* thought Josh.

Josh helped the kids into the old SUV, fastened them into their car seats, and off they went to Makena Bay. Josh wanted to kill two birds with one stone: entertain the kids and check for honu. Without waiting, the kids ran down to the bay, put on their snorkel masks and jumped into the water. Josh hurried to keep up with them. Without taking his eyes off his rambunctious kids, he took his t-shirt off and threw it into the sand along with three towels. Then he got into the water and patiently answered their onslaught of questions.

"Daddy, what's that one?" asked Kimo. "Is that a humuhumu fish?"

Josh laughed, but Kimo was right. "Yes, that's a humuhumunukunukuāpua'a. It's a bit hard to say. You could also call it a reef trigger fish. That's easier."

"Oh," said Kimo. "I like the long name. It's cool." He dove back down.

A honu swam in the distance. Josh was happy to see him. Both kids came up for air and asked, "Dad, can we go to the rocky beach over there and see if any honu are hanging out?"

Josh smiled. He had trained them well.

"Sure. I wanted to do that anyhow. Let's go and count them."

They dried off and put the beach towels around their shoulders as they walked over to the rocky cove. Kimo chased a chicken and fell on his knees.

"Owww!" he yelled. Tears streamed down his face.

"Let me see," Josh said, gently tugging Kimo's hands away from his knee. He howled louder when he saw the tiny drops of blood on the small abrasion. Since he had nothing else handy, Josh washed Kimo's knee off with some salt water and held him until the tears stopped.

"That's not bad at all, Kimo, be a brave guy. It'll stop bleeding in a second. Once we're back at the car, I'll put some Neosporin and a Band-Aid on it." Internally, he was cursing. Melanie would make a big deal out of it and blame him for letting her son get injured.

"Okay, let's leave the chickens alone. And please don't forget, guys. We need to keep a distance from the honu. We're not allowed to get too close or touch them. You know that, right?"

"Yes, Daddy," they said.

Josh took both kids by the hand. Two honu were basking in the sun on the rocks. One had a number etched into the side of his carapace which meant he had been a patient at the Turtle Rescue within the past year.

"Stay here kids. Don't get any closer or we'll scare the honu." He got his phone out to take a photo and some notes. "Can either of you read those numbers on the carapace to me? That way I can go back to my computer and check who he is and if he's been hanging around here before."

Alana squinted and read, "Zero eight dash two one."

"Very good." Josh took a photo and wrote down the number in his notes.

"Okay, do you want to go back to the car and have a snack now?"

Tired from swimming, both kids nodded. Josh typed the number into his phone, but again, it wasn't the honu from Ma'alaea Harbor.

Chapter 22

Old wooded plumeria trees and hibiscus shrubs lined Luana and Paul's driveway. Mark and Sienna rang the doorbell. They didn't want to just walk into the house even though they had a separate entrance and a key. After they rang a few times, a tall slender man in his early sixties with gray hair and bright blue eyes behind a pair of glasses opened the door. Renowned painter Paul Kent ran a paint-covered hand through his disheveled hair.

Mark introduced Sienna and himself, and he and Paul Kent shook hands. Sienna was starstruck.

"Mr. Kent, I can't even tell you how much I admire your work," she said. "I had no idea we were staying in your house."

Mark and Paul whipped their heads toward her. Mark had no idea Sienna could get starstruck since he didn't get excited over "celebrity" status. They were still just people.

"No worries," said Paul. "I'm a normal human being, I just enjoy painting. Luana does most of the work around here, I must admit. I'm not a good housekeeper at all."

Sienna held the beautiful flower arrangement up. "Well, she's quite talented too."

"Yes, that's true. She is an artist when it comes to creating beautiful bouquets. Come on in."

He led them into a bright studio at the back of the house. Sienna was beside herself seeing where Paul Kent worked and what he was working on. Paul and Mark got a big kick out of Sienna's enthusiasm. His tropical landscapes covered the two walls that weren't floor-to-ceiling windows. Several easels displayed paintings. A small canvas sat on an easel next to a table full of paints and brushes. He had obviously been working on this in his newer, more contemporary style. It was a honu.

"The studio is a bit crammed, but since my place out at Waioka Pond was broken into a couple of years ago, I can't keep paintings there anymore," he explained.

"I heard about that," replied Sienna. "I really like your newer style."

"Thank you." After a short moment of silence, he added, "Well, I came through here not only to show you what I'm working on but also because the other entrance to your room is right here." He opened a door leading to the back entrance of the mother-in-law suite. "If it's okay, I'd prefer if you used the other entrance. I'm easily distractable," he said grinning.

"Of course," they replied.

"And thank you very much for letting us stay here," Mark added.

"Palila's friends are our friends too," he replied.

———————⊃◦⊂———————

They retrieved their luggage and brought it into the sunny beautifully decorated mother-in-law suite. The ocean lined the house's backyard, which included a private terrace surrounded by lush tropical plants.

It was time for Mark to go see Palila. Mark paced the room, sporadically pulling things out of his duffel bag and putting them away to hide the nervousness of his actions.

"Hāmoa Beach is right past Lani and Max's house. Why don't you get your bathing suit on, walk over with me, and you can just go to the beach?"

Sienna planned to drive back to Kōkī Beach, then to Hāna to pick up some fruit at one of the stands and possibly hike up to Fagan's Cross, so he was on his own for now.

Mark walked the few hundred yards to Kōkī Beach House, the beautiful two-story house Lani had inherited a few years ago from her at-the-time unknown Aunt Malani. He wasn't sure if he should knock at the main entrance or the guesthouse on the right. Lani and Max were probably working, so he knocked on the guesthouse door. There was no answer. Then he rang the doorbell at the main house. Leila Kalekilio, Luana's mom and Lani's grandmother, opened the door.

"Someone has to be with Palila and the kids at all times," she explained after she had introduced herself. "Palila is waiting for you out in the backyard. Please follow me."

They walked through the house to a wooden terrace then through a big tropical backyard to the ocean. Palila sat in a comfortable armchair under some shady trees, her legs covered by her favorite quilt. The kids weren't far from her, swinging and sliding down a handmade wooden playset. Nalu kept a sharp eye on her mom.

Palila had declined even more in the past few days and

looked emaciated. She barely ate anymore. Her arms were just skin and bones. The honu tattoo she had gotten when they were together peeked out from her short sleeves. Her once high cheek bones were now too pronounced and made her look ghostly. She and Nalu had been nervous and excited to see Mark. As he stepped up to her, she smiled and said, "At least there's no better place to die than here, right?"

Mark cleared his throat, his eyes glassy with unshed tears as he sat down next to this woman who used to be the picture of health.

Palila couldn't bear the silence. "Remember us surfing back there at Kōkī Beach?"

She pointed to Alau Island in the distance. Mark finally had to smile.

"Yes, the day you surfed in that storm and scared Josh and I to death will never be forgotten. Even Nalu will tell her grandkids one day."

Palila flinched. She would never get to see Nalu grow up or meet her kids and grandkids. Palila changed the subject.

"So, will I meet Sienna?"

"Yes, if you want to. We didn't want to overwhelm you. We can talk today, and you can meet Sienna tomorrow."

Nalu realized Mark was here and ran up, excited, then stopped shy three feet in front of him. Kai and Paolo, Lani and Max's kids, followed Nalu and stopped behind her. All three stood there staring at Mark.

"Come say hi to Mark, guys," said Palila. "This is Nalu's dad. Mark, this is Paolo and Kai, and you know Nalu."

All three kids said, "Hi."

"Hey, kids. Hey, Nalu," said Mark.

Quietly, they said hi again and ran back to the swing set.

Mark and Palila laughed, but Palila's laugh turned into a cough. Mark panicked for a second. Then he jumped up to grab the water sitting on the little wicker table and handed it to her. He held on to it, helping her drink so she wouldn't spill it.

The water helped, but Palila breathed heavily and couldn't speak.

"Maybe you should lie down?" asked Mark. "I'm right over at Luana's house. I can come back anytime. Or I can hang out and watch the kids."

"Yes, could you help me to the guesthouse?" she asked and started coughing again. She drank another sip of water, slowly stood up and walked back to the guesthouse, supported by Mark.

"Maybe you can try and talk to Nalu," Palila rasped. "I don't know what to do about her. She should probably go with you since she shouldn't grow up without her father, but what if she refuses? She's as stubborn as me."

"Uh oh," he said, trying to be humorous again. "Get some rest. I'll go out and have a conversation with her."

Mark walked back outside and stopped at the swing set. He watched the kids take turns sliding, swinging and climbing up to a little tower like three little energizer bunnies.

He thought about what Palila said. A ten-year-old probably shouldn't decide where she lived and grew up. She might want one thing one day and change her mind the next. But then Palila was probably right. Could they force her to move to Florida where everyone was a stranger?

Nalu walked up to him and asked, "Do you want to play with us, Mark?"

"That's very nice of you, Nalu. I think the swing set would collapse if I tried to climb on it."

She laughed. "I think you're right. Shall we play something else? We could play hide 'n' seek!" She turned toward Kai and Paolo. "Guys, we're going to play hide 'n' seek with Mark. I'll start counting and you go hide." She leaned against the solid wall of the play set, counting as she held her hands in front of her eyes. Mark, Kai and Paolo ran in different directions, looking for places to hide. Mark hid behind Palila's chair down by the ocean.

"Ready or not, here I come!" yelled Nalu. She ran through the yard looking for everyone.

Mark made a loud "peep" as she ran by.

She stopped and slowly walked up to the chair. "I got you!" she yelled and tagged him. They both laughed.

"I'll help you look for the others." They looked on the terrace, the side of the house and the front, but they couldn't find them. They yelled for them to come out of their hiding places, "Come out, come out, wherever you are."

Leila came out when she heard them shouting.

"Paolo and Kai are inside having a snack."

Nalu folded her arms and said, "That doesn't count. That's cheating!"

With the other two kids inside, Mark took the opportunity for a private conversation.

"Nalu, do you think we could have a talk for a minute?"

"Sure," she said.

They walked over to Palila's favorite place by the water and sat down.

"I know we don't know each other very well," Mark started, "but could you imagine coming to Florida with me just to check it out?"

"No. I'm staying here," said Nalu. She started crying. That was exactly what she was afraid of when her mom died and left her alone. They all said he was her father, but she didn't want to leave Maui and go to Florida with a stranger she didn't even know.

Nalu ran to the house. Mark let her go. The attempt to talk had been a complete failure.

Chapter 23

Sienna drove back toward Hāna and stopped at Kōkī Beach. Mark had told her stories of him, Josh and Palila camping there with their friends. She walked under some low-hanging tree branches onto the beach. Alau Island, a beautiful little cone-shaped island, sat a quarter mile offshore. Two coconut palms had been planted at the top. One story said they were planted by star-crossed lovers. Another claimed there used to be three palms planted by soldiers who went to war. Two returned, one didn't.

Great frigatebirds danced around the island in the sky. Some surfers got pummeled by the rough waves. One of them succeeded and rode a big wave to shore.

Sienna envisioned Palila surfing there years ago, and her heart ached. Even though she hadn't met this woman yet, she had strong feelings for her and her daughter. Death and grief had wreaked havoc in her own life. Sienna had expected a lighthearted vacation. It wasn't turning out that way, but it was still a positive experience in many ways.

Sienna thought Mark might still love Palila, but she was sure it was a different kind of love. She still loved Ricky, her boyfriend from years ago even though he'd become involved with her sister. She'd always love him, but not the way she loved Mark. She wasn't sure how she'd handle seeing Mark with Palila, but she'd take one step at a time.

Sienna shook off the sad thoughts and watched a family picnic in the dark red sand. She read in her travel guide:

"Legend says the dark red sand was produced by the nearby cinder cone hill of Ka Iwi O Pele, meaning 'bones of Pele.' According to Hawaiian legend, Kōkī Beach is where the volcano goddess Pele fought her final battle with her older sister, Namakoakaha'i, the goddess of the ocean. Pele's bones were stacked along the Kōkī shoreline, and her spirit traveled to Kilauea of the Big Island."

As she walked back to the Jeep, Sienna realized that people were sitting everywhere, eating. She discovered a food stand under some pop-up tents. A sign said *Huli Chicken*. A man stood over a grill, basting big chicken breasts with some sort of marinade and turning them from time to time. Sienna's mouth watered. She got in line and ordered a plate. Then she sat down at one of the picnic tables and enjoyed the sweet, tangy chicken, Hawaiian macaroni salad and rice. She hadn't realized how hungry she was. *What a heavenly place this is,* thought Sienna. *No wonder it's called Heavenly Hāna.*

When she was done, she drove up the hill toward the Hāna Highway. Her mobile phone beeped. Tom's name flashed across her screen, but she didn't bother looking at the message while driving through such a hilly area. Grassy cow pastures lined the road.

These must be the happiest cows in the world, Sienna thought as she looked across the lush fields down to the ocean. She stopped at the food trucks and Hāna Farms' fruit stand on the left. Two college students stood behind the table. One took care of a customer, the other one skillfully cut up a pineapple.

"Would you like to try a piece?" asked the young man as Sienna walked up to the stand.

"Sure." Sienna took the offered piece and popped it into her mouth. It was sweet as candy. Enticed by all the exotic fruits and vegetables, she bought more than she could carry. The two young men helped her to her car. They handed her a flyer.

Every Friday pizza & live music at Hāna Farms: 6-9 pm

"That's today. You're lucky you're in town," said the first young man. "It's at the first stand you pass when you drive into town, across from Waianapanapa State Park."

"Thanks," said Sienna smiling. "We'll try to make it."

She pulled her phone from her back pocket and tucked the flier in its place. When she looked at the time, a reminder for Tom's text popped up.

I hope all is well. I had to come to Hāna to take care of something for my sister-in-law who lives here. Aren't you here too? Want to go hiking at Waianapanapa State Park? I have a reservation at 2 pm before I head back to Kihei.

Sienna hesitated. Her heart pounded faster. One time had been okay to meet Tom secretly, but twice? She was heading into dangerous territory, but she'd enjoy hiking and talking with Tom again. She'd also need a reservation to enter Waianapanapa State Park, and she didn't have one. It was 1:30, so perfect timing.

She replied, *Sure. Where shall I meet you?*

I can pick you up at the hotel.

Okay. I think I'm less than five minutes away.

189

Me too! See you soon.

Sienna hated admitting it to herself, but she was excited to see Tom again. Things with him were so easygoing. She tried to tell herself she wasn't doing anything wrong. What was going to happen? She parked in the hotel parking lot. Tom drove up, as she got out of the Jeep.

"Aloha," he said brightly.

"Aloha." Sienna got into his car.

He pointed up the hill beyond the parking lot. "Can you see that cross up there? That's Fagan's Cross. You should try to hike up there for sunrise while you're here. It's spectacular."

The big cross had been built in honor of Paul Fagan who established cattle ranching and opened the first hotel in Hāna in 1946.

"That's actually what I was going to do right now," she replied. "But, good point, sunrise would be much nicer."

Tom took a left onto the Hāna Highway. "You should also go and tour the hotel, it's very nice," he said. He pointed to the right. "And down there is Hāna Bay, the little hole-in-the-wall place has some good breakfast sandwiches, if it's still open."

In less than ten minutes, they arrived at Waianapanapa State Park. As they drove into the entrance, Tom asked, "Did you know that Wai'anapanapa means 'glistening water?'"

Tom presented his reservation to the parking attendants who, to Sienna's surprise, greeted him like an old friend and showed him where to park.

"Let's go down to the black sand beach first, and then we can hike a little down this way which is actually a part of the old King's Highway," he said, pointing to the right.

"Oh, the King's Highway? Could we do that first? I would really love to see the original blue rocks in the middle of the path. In La Perouse I never saw any traces of them."

"You can only see them if you really know where to look," he answered. "The spots I've seen them in La Perouse were further inland than where we were. The Hāna part is a four-mile stretch between Pailoa Bay by the airport to Kainalimu Bay in Hāna. There are more than twenty-five ancient sites. One of the paths leads down to the ruins of a heiau, an old Hawaiian temple."

Tom led Sienna to the trailhead.

"Originally, five hundred years ago, the King's Highway circumnavigated the entire island of Maui. It was a vital trade route built by indigenous Hawaiians but rebuilt in the 1800s by prisoners."

The hike followed jagged coastline and cliffs and crossed lava flows. They climbed narrow paths of big lava rocks surrounded by lush tropical rainforest.

Sienna stopped to catch her breath when the rocks got slippery. Tom turned around and grabbed her hand to pull her up. He pulled her a little too hard, and she almost landed in his arms. They both held their breath and pulled back, afraid to touch each other, then laughed off their silliness.

Sienna enjoyed the beautiful views and the company. Their conversation was about history, geography and botany, not about cancer or dying people. She felt selfish but enjoyed the distraction.

Tom pointed out a few of the original blue rocks from the King's Highway. Sienna was elated to see this much raw history, and she cheered, "Yah, this is really exciting. Thanks so much for bringing me here!" She hugged him. Again, the chemistry between them crackled, but they were determined to prove they could be just friends.

"It's probably time to turn around if we want to go the other way to the black sand beach and see the lava tube. It's definitely worth it."

After taking a big sip of cool, refreshing water from their metal canisters, they turned around, following the jagged coastline past the parking lot. They passed a blowhole and looked out at the beautiful sea arches and palm trees growing along the water's edge, wherever they had enough space to root between the lava rocks. Tom pointed out some gray birds with white heads and orange feet darting through the sky and walking along the ledges.

"You can find the largest colony of Hawaiian noddies here at the park. They're a common Hawaiian bird that nests in the caves and rocky ledges."

A cemetery overlooked the coast on their left. They almost bumped into a woman stepping out of the enclosed area. It was Lani. She had brought flowers to put on her Aunt Malani's grave.

Sienna felt like she'd been caught red-handed hiking here with another man while Mark sat at Palila's side.

"Hey, Sienna! I'm glad you're getting to explore the area a bit. It's a beautiful place."

"Hey, Lani, this is my, um, friend Tom."

"Oh, I know Tom. Katherine was a good friend of mine, and her sister still is. Hāna's a small town," she said grinning.

"Hey, Tom. How do you guys know each other?"

"We first ran into each other hiking at La Perouse, and today I realized that we're both in Hāna. So, I asked Sienna if she'd join me hiking out here," replied Tom who came up with an answer quicker than Sienna.

Lani's smile wavered for a second at his response.

"Well, I just brought some flowers to my Aunt Malani's grave. I'd better get going. Luana's waiting for me. Will we see you at dinner later, Sienna?"

"Yes, I'll be there."

"Okay, see you later. Bye, Tom, good to see you. Are you having dinner at Kelly's, or do you want to come over too?"

"Thanks, but I have to head back to Kihei now, I just came over to help Kelly with something in the house."

"Okay, drive careful." And Lani was gone.

The encounter dampened Sienna's mood. She was going to have some explaining to do later.

They continued to a flight of stairs leading down to the black sand beach, checked out the lava tube and hiked out to the overlook with views of the entire state park, but Sienna couldn't enjoy herself anymore. Tom noticed it.

"I'm sorry if I got you in trouble. I should have known that Hāna is a small town, and everyone knows me. I had no idea that we'd run into Lani of all people. But it's not like we're breaking a law or cheating on Mark. Maybe you could tell him about me and that we're just friends?"

"Yeah," she replied, subdued. "I think I've just made things worse by not telling him."

—————◦◦—————

Palila was back in her armchair down by the water, watching a juvenile honu that had been coming to hang out on the smooth rocks next to her and just stared at her. The honu's presence calmed Palila down immensely. She slowly fell into a light sleep and started dreaming...

In her dream, she felt herself transforming into a honu. Her arms and legs became short and scaly and turned into shorter flippers. Her back felt heavy as a carapace grew on it, her hair disappeared and her head became more streamlined as it turned into the head of a green sea turtle. Palila felt awkward and heavy as she slowly crawled down the lava rock toward the warm water and became engulfed by the ocean. The other honu was waiting for her in the waves. She stretched her flippers and felt their power as she swam through the waves, following the other honu. Her body now felt weightless as she dove deeper and deeper, swimming along the coast toward Hāmoa Beach. She could hold her breathe just like a honu, as her new friend led her through the water. She felt like she was flying as she darted through the water. She hadn't been this carefree and pain free in a while. The water became more shallow as they swam toward the beach and watched some children play in the waves. It was Nalu, Kai and Paolo. Palila's heart became warm as she watched her daughter play in the waves with her friends. The children discovered the two honu and dove down toward them, aware that they had to keep a safe distance of ten feet. The honu played, darting toward them, swimming around them, and the kids laughed as the honu chased them. Finally, the kids became tired and let the waves carry them ashore where Max was patiently waiting for them.

"We just saw two honu that were playing with us," Nalu told Max full of excitement.

Kai chimed in. "They kept swimming toward us and then swam away. It was like they wanted to play chase with us."

"I can't wait to tell my mom about them, she loves honu," said Nalu.

Max smiled and nodded. "Make sure you always respect them and keep a safe distance of about ten feet, okay guys?"

They all nodded.

"And make sure you never go deeper than your waist. There can be some dangerous undertows back there where the water gets deeper." He pointed out toward the west side of the beach.

They all nodded again and looked out one more time, checking whether they could see the two honu, but they were gone.

———◦———

Palila slowly woke up as she heard the kids, chattering excitedly, running toward her through the backyard. Kai and Paolo stayed back a few feet in a shy and respectful manner, but Nalu ran up to her, jumping up and down full of excitement.

Palila's dream had felt so real, that she briefly ran her hands up and down her arms to feel if she had flippers. Her skin felt unusually rough but became softer as she was fully awake now.

"Mom," said Nalu enthusiastically, "we just saw two honu

at Hāmoa Beach that played with us! It was so much fun, they kept chasing us, wanting us to chase them back."

Palila did a double take. That was exactly what she'd done in her dream... was it a dream or not? She'd have to tell Ana about this later.

She smiled and gave Nalu a hug. "That's nice, honey. I'm glad you're having fun."

Chapter 24

Sienna had just enough time to take a shower and walk over to Lani and Max's house for dinner. Lani and Max were in the kitchen making spaghetti and meatballs. Luana set the table, and Paul hung out with the kids in the living room.

Mark sat hunched over the kitchen counter nursing a drink.

Sienna stepped up to him and gave him a quick hug, whispering, "Mark, you don't look so good. Was it bad?"

"Well, it was as to be expected with Palila, but it was quite bad with Nalu. I don't think she'll even consider coming to Florida with us."

"Maybe she just needs some time," replied Sienna. "Remember what she's going through right now. And she barely knows you."

"Yeah, but there's no time for us to get to know each other. I need to be back at work in Ma'alaea Harbor on Monday, and afterwards, I'm only staying three more weeks."

"Maybe you'll have to stay longer. I'm sure you can discuss a leave of absence with the Turtle Sanctuary. This is important."

"I'll see if I can get through to her when I get a chance."

Mark thanked her and gave her a kiss, looking deep into

her eyes. "So, how was your day?"

She took a sip of his wine. Max noticed she didn't have anything to drink and asked, "Would you like your own glass of wine, Sienna?"

"Yes, sure. Thanks," she replied.

She wanted to tell Mark about Tom, especially now that Lani had seen them, but there were too many people around. So she replied to Mark's question as best she could.

"It was great. I heard about some live music at Hāna Farms tonight. It's only once a week on Fridays. We should go."

"I'm not sure if I'm in the mood for that."

"Well, let's play it by ear and see how we feel after dinner."

Max had poured Sienna a glass of wine and set it down on the counter. "Mahalo," she said, taking a sip. She walked over to Paul and the kids and asked, "May I?" before she sat down on the couch.

Kai and Paulo didn't know this lady. They continued playing with their toy cars more quietly than before.

Paul introduced Sienna. "Kids, have you met Miss Sienna? She's from a really nice place in Florida called the Keys and lives at a turtle sanctuary. She can tell you a lot about sea turtles, just like Mr. Mark."

Kai and Paolo turned their attention toward Sienna and started asking questions. Nalu was hesitant at first, but she loved sea turtles and honu more than anything else.

"How come you live in a turtle sanctuary?"

"Do you live right with the turtles, like next to their basins, or do they live in your house?"

"Do you have the same honu just like the ones here?"

Sienna patiently answered all their questions and treated them like grown-ups. She had always treated children that way and was loved and respected in return. Soon, all three kids were trying to sit on her lap at the same time. They hung from her words as she told them about her families' adventures in the Keys, the crunching parrotfish, the Hemingway cats and the valuable pink conch pearls she had found in her sister's office that had saved the turtle sanctuary.

Max and Lani called everyone over for dinner. All the kids wanted to sit next to Sienna. Mark was astounded. That was why he loved her so much. Lani and Sienna made sure Mark sat on the other side of Nalu, and soon Sienna had Mark involved in the conversation about sea creatures, hurricanes and key lime pie. Nalu proudly told her friends that Mark was a sea turtle specialist and had come here to help rescue the honu, her favorite animals, and that Mark lived at the sea turtle sanctuary in Florida with Sienna and their kids.

"Why didn't you bring your kids?" Nalu asked, eager to meet them.

"They have school," replied Mark, "and my daughter Sydney stays with her mother sometimes."

"So, is Sydney my sister?" asked Nalu.

"Yes, she's your little sister in Florida."

Nalu stared off, thinking about her unknown sister and how much fun it would be to meet her.

The dinner ran its course. Everyone laughed and talked and had a great time. They were all still sitting around the table when Lani asked Mark, "I have to check on Palila and give her some company. Do you want to join me?"

"Sure," he said and got up. They walked out through the dark garden. Nalu followed them out.

"I wanna come and say good night to Mom too," she said, catching up with Mark and walking close to him. Whether to be close to Mark or keep a close eye on him, she wasn't sure.

"Of course, you can come, Nalu," Lani said.

"Did you know that honu swim all the way to the French Frigate Shoals to lay their eggs?" Nalu asked her as she walked next to them.

"Oh, really? I had no idea," Lani responded. "Did you know that honu can be guardian spirits, 'aumakua, for families?"

"No, I didn't know that."

"It's true. Your mom wishes to come back as a honu after she dies."

Nalu looked at Lani with big eyes.

"Every time you see a honu after your mom is gone, it should remind you of her. It might be her saying hi and watching over you from wherever she is."

Nalu nodded. She liked that. Mark liked it too, he smiled at Lani thankfully.

Palila slept peacefully in the hospital bed set up by the window so she could see the ocean and the stars. They tried not to wake her up, but her ears still worked quite well, and she opened her eyes to two little slits.

"Hey sweetheart," she said to Nalu Her voice was hoarse. Nalu took her hand and caressed her mother's cheek with her other.

"Would you like me to make you some tea?" asked Lani.

"No, I'm too tired," Palila whispered. It took all her strength to lift her arm up to her daughter's head and caress her. "But I'm never too tired to say hi to my sweet Nalu."

"Mommy, Lani said you might come back as a honu when you're dead. Is that true?"

"Yes, I hope so, and I'll watch over you." Then she fell asleep again.

Lani pulled Mark aside, a catch in her throat, as she whispered, "Ana's daughter is bringing her over tomorrow morning, and she might stay for the next few days. In other words, it might only be a few more days."

Mark ran a hand down his face. Tears filled his eyes, but he didn't let them fall in front of Nalu. He needed to be strong for her.

Lani put a comforting hand on Nalu's shoulder. "Nalu, you don't want to go to bed yet, do you? You can play with Kai and Paolo for another hour while I clean up, then I'll come and sleep here with you and your mom, okay?"

Nalu nodded and turned the baby monitor back on. Palila couldn't be left alone anymore. They walked back to the house while Palila slept with calm but shallow breaths.

Paul and Luana left after Lani and Nalu went back over to the guesthouse and the cleanup was done. Mark and Sienna joined them for the short walk down Haneo'o Road to their house. The visibility of the stars was incredible since there were barely any lights around. They walked along, pointing out the various constellations.

It was too early for bed when they arrived at the house. Sienna remembered the live music at Hāna Farms.

"Do you guys ever go to the live music and dinner at Hāna Farms on Friday evenings?" she asked Paul and Luana.

"Yes, we've been there. You guys should go. You'll still have about an hour to enjoy the music. It's very cool slack key guitar," said Paul. "I'd go with you if I didn't have to get up early tomorrow. I want to finish my painting, and my best light in the studio is in the morning."

"Shall we go for a drink?" Sienna asked Mark.

He hesitated, not really in the mood, then he nodded since Sienna really wanted to go. They went inside to freshen up for a few minutes, jumped into the Jeep and drove down Haneo'o Road toward Hāna.

The venue, an open-air building built of giant bamboo canes, had already significantly emptied out, but a few people still sat there finishing dinner, drinking and listening to the two locals playing slack guitar.

"They sound really good!" exclaimed Sienna as she sat down at a table in the corner.

"It looks like self-serve. Would you like a beer?" asked Mark.

"That would be great." He waked up to the counter and ordered two Bikini Blonde lagers.

They sat and enjoyed the soothing music and the cool breeze of the trade winds.

Soon the musicians finished playing and started packing up their instruments. With the relative quiet and privacy, Sienna decided to tell Mark about Tom. Just as she opened her mouth, one of the musicians yelled, "Hey, Mark!" He walked over. "Remember me? It's Chris! We used to hang out at Kōkī Beach."

Mark recognized him, and they gave each other a big bear hug. He introduced Sienna, and after getting another beer, they reminisced about old times until the place closed. Sienna sat there listening, enjoying that Mark was upbeat again having this conversation with Chris.

But she didn't get a chance to tell him about Tom.

Chapter 25

A wave rolled in, thundering loudly. Iwa birds fluttered across the sky dipped in streaks of pink and gray. The sun rose through clouds above the horizon. The clouds burned off, a new day on Maui was born. The sun climbed higher over the beach on Honoapiilani Highway. As the next wave pulled back, a couple of honu crawled ashore to bask in the morning sun.

A lonely young fisherman sat in a folding chair on the beach, not far from the honu. Another fisherman walked up and sat down close to the first one, a rather handsome guy who didn't really look like a fisherman.

"Where you from?" asked the second fisherman. "You not from around here?"

"No, visiting from Lana'i. How's business around here?

"Not great at all. I haven't been catching much. I need some money, man. My wife needs surgery, and our copay is through the roof."

"Hey, can I trust you, brah?" said the first fisherman. "I know a quick way to make some serious cash."

"Yeah, sure, I appreciate it. We need a wonder or something."

The first fisherman checked if anyone was within earshot, but they were the only ones on the beach this early.

"There's this guy who's paying top dollar for honu. Bring them to my boat, 'Lana'i Princess', slip twenty-seven, at Ma'alaea Harbor on Monday. My boss will pay you five thousand dollars. It needs to be before sunrise. The honu must be unharmed and of course in some type of container so you can't see it. And keep this to yourself."

"Thanks, man, I'll see what I can do. What's your name?" asked the second fisherman. He prepared his fishing pole and cast it into the water.

"Steve. If I'm not there, ask for Ryan. He's the big boss's assistant and my boss."

After a while, the first fisherman left. "Have a great day, brah," he shouted as he walked back up the beach.

"You too, I'll try to see you on Monday."

Steve threw a shaka, got in a big shiny truck and drove away with screeching tires.

The second fisherman got a walkie-talkie out of one of his buckets. "Jon Jon for Michael. Come in, Michael."

"Michael for Jon Jon. I'm listening."

"I've got some info for O'Shen and headquarters..."

The news was forwarded to O'Shen. She informed Josh who was out walking the dogs with his kids.

"Great news in the honu case. We got some info about a boat in Ma'alaea Harbor and a honu delivery early Monday morning. Please don't discuss this with anyone yet."

"Awesome."

"We'll continue keeping an eye on all the beaches until

then."

"Thanks, O'Shen."

He was about to end the call when she asked, "Oh, Josh, I need a date for a function at Mama's tomorrow evening. My boyfriend can't make it. He's in Honolulu. Wanna come?"

Josh grinned. He didn't mind being a fill-in date at Mama's Fish House if he got a free meal there, and he liked O'Shen's sometimes-abrasive, straightforward manner. They'd been friends since O'Shen started working at the Wailuku Police Station.

"Sure," he replied. "Is it formal? And what time? I have to drop the kids back off at five."

"It's black tie, and it starts at six thirty, so you'll be right on time."

"Okay, see you then.

Sienna walked down Hāmoa Beach. The sunrise bathed the sky and sand in red, orange and pink. Sienna couldn't sleep and had snuck out of the suite to be alone for a little bit before she met Palila after breakfast. Just thinking of it made Sienna's heart race. She took deep breaths to calm her anxiety.

The hills behind Hāmoa Beach reminded her of what Lani had told her yesterday. A developer had recently tried to buy the land behind the beach to build oceanfront condos, and the town of Hāna had been able to overrule his petition because Lani's basset hound Lilly had found traces of an ancient burial site. How amazing that the dog had saved the day after getting in trouble and running away. Oceanfront condos would've destroyed the entire area.

Sienna listened to the roaring ocean as the waves moved in and out like a cathartic heartbeat. She turned around at the end of the beach and, not paying attention for a second, got splashed by a big wave crashing ashore. Forgetting everything, she screamed with glee and jumped back, simply enjoying the moment. She tasted salty droplets on her lips and wiped the sea spray from her face.

It felt good and refreshing, so she didn't care that her shirt and shorts had gotten wet. The wind picked up as it started raining. She didn't care about this either and kept marching along the beach in the opposite direction until she was back at the stairs. By the time she was back, it was just drizzling a little.

Max came down the stairs, his surfboard under his arm.

"Aloha, Sienna. Oh, you're all wet, do you want to use my towel?"

"Hey, Max. Mahalo. It's okay. I'm sure by the time I'm home, I'll be dry again."

"Well, I'm trying to get my half hour of surfing in before everybody wakes up," he said, waving at her as he jogged toward the water.

"Have fun." She decided to watch him a little before she headed back.

Max walked toward the ocean, threw his surfboard over the first wave break, then himself onto the board and paddled out. He watched the waves until a big one formed behind him, and he paddled hard as the wave broke, catapulting him ahead. He stood up at the perfect moment and rode his surfboard all the way ashore, crouching his strong legs, holding his arms out for balance.

Sienna envisioned Palila surfing as a young woman. A Palila she hadn't even met yet but heard how athletic and strong she had been. How strong she was still. Her eyes filled with tears again as she watched Max paddle out one more time but saw Palila in her imagination...

Sienna walked home through the drizzling rain. The clouds disappeared, and the sparkling sun came out. A rainbow appeared on the oceanside behind the houses. *Maybe there was always a little bit of hope,* she thought. Mark was waiting for her and opened the door as she was about to step in.

"I was just about to send the search troops out for you," he joked. "I was worried. You forgot your cell phone."

"Yeah, sorry, I was trying to be quiet and realized I didn't have it when I was already past Lani's house. I just went for a walk down to the beach. I couldn't sleep all night."

Mark took Sienna in his arms with tears in his eyes and kissed her head as they both took shaky breaths. He hadn't slept well either.

They drank some coffee and ate a few bites of banana bread until it was time to go see Palila. As they walked, Sienna thought, *Now would be the time to tell Mark about Tom.* But it might make him feel even worse. Would there ever be a good time?

Mark walked in front of Sienna along the road to make room for passing cars. Their hands touched, as if to give each other strength.

When they reached the guesthouse, Mark squeezed Sienna's hand one more time and gave her a kiss before stepping in.

Ana had just given Palila some tea and meditated with her. Palila was too weak to get up today. She lay in her hospital bed, covered with her favorite quilt though it was warm inside.

Shallow breaths puffed through her cracked lips. Though she shivered from cold, pearls of sweat beaded on her forehead. Mark and Sienna walked up to her.

"Palila, this is Sienna," he whispered. He knew Palila wanted to speak with Sienna alone, so he added, "Ana and I will give you guys some privacy now. Sienna can let us know if you need anything."

"Aloha, Palila, nice to meet you," said Sienna, sitting on a chair next to the bed.

"Thanks for coming," Palila rasped. "And sorry for ruining your vacation." She coughed a little.

"Please, don't worry about that. Let me get you something to drink." Sienna grabbed a cup of water with a lid and a straw that stood on a side table and held it up to Palila who gratefully sipped it.

"Mahalo." Palila examined Sienna's face. "You look like a nice person." She paused to catch her breath. "It seems Mark loves you very much. He told me he proposed to you." Sienna let her talk. "I never had a father." She paused again, gathering the energy to continue. "And Nalu didn't either. That's why I'd really like her to go to Florida with you guys and grow up with her father. Do you think you can help me with that?" she asked.

"Of course, I can. She seems very interested in seeing the sea turtles and meeting her half-sister. Maybe that's how we can get her to come with us."

Palila searched for Sienna's hand and squeezed it.

"Mahalo nui loa. Thank you very much. And please try to let her visit her old home as often as she can so she doesn't forget about her heritage and culture. I know flights are expensive but—" She coughed again. Sienna tried to hand her the cup again, but this time she couldn't stop. The cough shook her frail body, and Sienna thought she might start choking. She panicked and went to get Ana.

"Ana, I think we need some help here. Palila can't stop coughing."

Ana brought a cup of Palila's herbal tea and, with Ana's support, drank a few sips and stopped coughing. With Palila calm, Ana left the room. She took Sienna's hand and just said "Mahalo. You're a good woman, and Mark is a good man."

Sienna barely held back the tears, but she stayed strong for Palila. "I'll take care of her like my own daughter," she said. "Don't worry."

"Thank you." Palila closed her eyes and fell asleep again. Her breathing deepened and relaxed, her face grew softer. Meeting and talking to Sienna had been so important to her. But it exhausted her, and now that she had said what she wanted to say, she could finally relax.

Chapter 26

After a nice lunch at the huli huli chicken stand at Kōkī Beach with Sienna, Mark went back to hang out with Palila. She felt a bit more energetic again. They sat at her favorite spot underneath the trees by the ocean. She felt at peace here, looking out at the water. The juvenile honu from her dreams was sitting on a big lava rock, looking at her from time to time as if watching over her. Lani, Luana and Ana were certain that he and Palila were somehow communicating with each other. The men all thought they were crazy, but they had no better explanation for the honu showing up and hanging out by Palila's side every time she was there.

Mark held more a monologue than had a conversation with Palila because even speaking had become a huge effort for her. But she loved listening to the old stories Mark told her.

"Remember the one time we were staying in Hāna, went upcountry for the day and ran out of gas?" asked Mark, laughing.

Palila smiled and nodded. Of course, she remembered.

"Remember? It got dark and we had to hitchhike to the next gas station in Makawao? There were no cars on the road at all, until two shady looking guys stopped. They looked like drug dealers, and their car smelled like weed."

They both chuckled.

"Then we had to walk back to the car because there was no traffic again, and of course, no taxis or uber. We got back to Hāna after midnight, exhausted and starving."

They both laughed with tears in their eyes. In hindsight, it was a great memory, and they could laugh about the adventure.

"Remember the time we camped in the Makawao Forest Reserve, and it rained so hard we couldn't leave the tent all day?"

Palila nodded. She was tired again, maybe in pain, and her eyes were closed. Mark's eyes filled with tears. They had some great memories. He wondered how his life would have been if he had stayed in Maui with her. It was a moot point though. And he wouldn't have Sydney or have met Sienna.

———————◦———————

Sienna, Ana and the kids drove to the area around Waioka Pond to find some medicinal herbs Ana needed for Palila's teas.

They climbed through a cattle gate. Since this seemed to be private property, Sienna asked, "Are we allowed to come here?"

"Yes, I have permission from the owners to come here and collect herbs. I'm older than dirt, and I assisted with the births of all of their kids and grandkids," she said grinning. "They owe me."

They walked down a dirt path and came up to the ruins of an old Portuguese oven, which Portuguese immigrants had built and used for baking bread more than a hundred years ago.

Instead of taking a right toward the rugged cliffs of Waioka Pond, they kept walking straight toward Paul's former studio, an old cottage on the ocean.

Drawn to the cottage, the kids looked through the windows and tried to open the door, but it was locked.

"This would be a great playhouse," Kai said, and Nalu nodded.

They gave up trying to get in after a while and ran ahead, picking flowers to bring back to Sienna and Ana as they all hiked along the rugged cliffs. Meadows flourished with blossoming flowers and crooked, wind-beaten monkeypod trees and jacarandas that bloomed the prettiest pastel purple in the spring.

As Nalu ran up with another big bunch of flowers, Ana said, "Malama 'āina, Nalu, take care of the land. Don't pick more flowers than we need. Others want some too, and they won't grow anymore if we pick them all."

Nalu looked down at the ground, ashamed. Ana noticed and added quickly, "But these are beautiful, mahalo nui loa. We can make leis with them."

She put the flowers in her basket and pointed at a few plumerias. "Go and pick up some blooms that have fallen off the trees, those are good for leis. But then come back, I want to show you some herbs over there." She pointed at some shrubs. "You need to start learning about the healing powers of the plants."

Ana and Sienna walked as the kids collected plumeria blooms. Ana stopped in front of a tree. "This is what we're looking for. It's māmaki, usually a large shrub or small tree. Look at the broad light-green leaves, the whitish undersides and green veins. The veins can also be pink or reddish. We can make a good strengthening tea for Palila with the fresh leaves. They're used for general weakness from illness."

Ana picked leaves. Sienna followed her example and helped.

"Okay, that's enough. We don't want too much. I'd rather come back and get fresh leaves. They'll just wilt."

The kids ran up, and Ana showed them the leaves and explained their medicinal powers.

"We also want to look for some noni leaves. They grow as a small tree or shrub as well. The leaves are long and glossy on the top side. I can add those to the tea. They have lots of vitamins and are anti-inflammatory." She kept walking.

"I remember a noni tree somewhere around here." And she was right. She picked a leaf and showed Sienna and the kids.

"Smell the ammonia scent," she said. "They don't smell or taste very good, but they're very healthy."

They wrinkled their noses as they smelled. None of them would be drinking noni tea anytime soon.

"That's all we need for now. I have everything else in my garden. Shall we have our picnic now?"

The girls and Paolo cheered as Sienna spread out a blanket on the grass and unpacked sandwiches, banana bread, cut fruit, carrot sticks and cherry tomatoes from her backpack. They ate by the oceanside. Noisy mynah birds chattered close by in a tree, probably hoping the humans would leave some crumbs.

"Don't leave any food lying around. Those mynah birds

can be obnoxious," said Ana just as Paolo dropped a piece of banana bread. A mynah bird flew up and snatched it away.

"Do we have a little more time?" Sienna quietly asked Ana.

Ana raised her eyebrows and nodded. She wondered what Sienna was up to. Sienna took a book out of her backpack and showed it to the kids. Ana understood.

"I brought a book about honu that I found in my room in your grandparents' house. Would you like me to read it to you?" asked Sienna.

They all yelled, "Yes!" and sat down around Sienna as she opened the book. The kids hung from her lips. Paolo crawled on her lap as she read about a honu that swam all the way to the French Frigate Shoals to lay its eggs. The girls crowded around her to see the illustrations. "Mark told me about the French Frigate Shoals," said Nalu, proud that she already knew about this story.

Ana sat a few yards away, meditating as she hummed a quiet chant.

After they packed up, Nalu walked close to Sienna on the hike back to the car, asking her questions about honu and the sea turtle sanctuary in Florida.

As they were passing Hāmoa Beach on the way back, Ana asked Sienna to park the car.

"I want to show you guys one of our ancient fish ponds."

They got out, walked along a path leading down to the ocean and came upon ancient lava rock walls that had been built into the shallow water close to shore.

"There used to be over two thousand fishponds like this in Hawaii, but most of them were abandoned. Now there are only about fifty," explained Ana. "But they still work. A stone wall like this was built in the shallow water. The fish would be washed in with a wave. Small fish could escape, but larger fish couldn't get back out. So, then every three years the residents would get together and harvest the fish. It was already done like this a thousand years ago. I'd like you guys to come to the next harvest with your parents. Max used to come but he's gotten so busy. Now that you guys are getting bigger, I think you should all come together."

The kids as well as Sienna were very impressed. There was such an abundance of Hawaiian history around Hāna.

———⊷∘⊶———

Palila fell into another deep sleep. Again, she dreamed of swimming through the ocean as a honu, happy and free of pain. When she woke up, she asked Ana, who was back to care for her, about her vivid dreams as a honu.

Ana smiled and replied, "I think that's a good sign. I've heard that before dying, many people experience vivid and meaningful dreams. They bring about a sense of peace, a change in perspective or an acceptance of death. Maybe your wish to become a honu will really come true if you want it hard enough."

———⊷∘⊶———

Mark decided to make use of the break and take Sienna for a drive. They headed away from Hāna down the winding road along the coast toward Haleakalā State Park. Mark wanted to show Sienna the Bamboo Forest and Waimoku Falls. The road was sketchier than The Road to Hāna. Two lanes turned into one. Cars could barely pass each other. In some spots there were no guardrails. Sienna thanked her guardian angel as they inched past another car. The crowns of the gigantic African tulip trees and monstera leaves scraped the Jeep's doors as they drove through a hairpin curve with sweeping ocean vistas.

A shrine had been built for someone who had died here. Someone had left fresh flowers at a cross with a picture and some candles sitting on the rocks.

A waterfall tumbled down the mountain into a turquoise pool. They stopped in a parking lot and walked across the street to hike down the path leading to the waterfall. An artist had set up a stand to sell her paintings, mostly depicting orchids and plumerias.

"Hey, Laura! Do you remember me?" asked Mark. "This is my girlfriend, Sienna."

"Aloha, Mark, aloha, Sienna. What'cha doing here? I haven't seen you in ages!"

"I came to work at the Maui Turtle Rescue in Ma'alaea, and then I ran into Palila. You know about her, don't you?"

"Yes, it's so sad. Everybody in Hāna and the surrounding areas knows. I'm visiting her tomorrow to say goodbye. Everyone is," she replied with tears in her eyes.

"Well, maybe we'll see you tomorrow. We're staying at Lani's parents' place."

"I love your paintings," said Sienna. "How much is this one?" she asked, pointing at a matted print of rainbow plumerias.

"Fifty, but for you thirty-five," replied Laura smiling.

"I'd really like one as a souvenir." Sienna looked for her wallet in her backpack.

"Let me get it," said Mark. "I'd like to get it for you as a gift." He got his wallet out and paid Laura.

After saying thank you and goodbye to Laura, they took pictures at the waterfall and walked back to the Jeep.

They drove past massive poinsettia shrubs and a sign that said *Pigs Crossing. Sienna* looked around for pigs but couldn't find any. They needed a day of fun and distraction. The lush countryside felt like the "real" old Hawaii. Finally, they passed a sign that said *Haleakalā State Park,* another one said *Kīpahulu - Ka 'Āina O Ka Makani Ka'ili Aloha – Land of the Love-Snatching Wind.*

"Kīpahulu is a moku, a traditional district or land division," explained Mark. "The purpose of moku signage is to remind people of the traditional land system, so travelers on the Hāna Highway know when they're entering a new district and understand that people here are still practicing the ancient culture and lifestyles."

They parked, put on their hiking shoes and walked across the street to the head of Pipiwai Trail. The trail started with steep rocks, like natural stairs. They took a break at a massive banyan tree and drank some cold, refreshing water. A steep abyss dropped behind the banyan tree. The stream had formed a gulch over countless millennia leading down to the Pools of 'Ohe'o, also known as the Seven Sacred Pools. A sign said, *Danger – keep out.*

The trail continued upward, along the gulch. Sienna discovered some delicious strawberry guava and picked some to share with Mark. A welcome snack along the way.

They walked over a bridge crossing the gulch and into a cool shady bamboo forest that continued for half a mile. The dense, endless canes touched each other in the gentle breeze and sounded like a thousand wooden wind chimes.

Mark and Sienna kept walking out of the bamboo forest and crossed a stream to the most magnificent cascading waterfall: four-hundred-foot-tall Waimoku Falls. They walked as close as they could. Mark wanted to take a selfie but realized his phone died.

"Can I use your phone to take some pictures?" he asked Sienna.

"Sure."

She stood next to him, and he took a few selfies of the two of them and then a few photos of just the waterfall. As Mark checked the photos, he swiped too far back and landed on some of Sienna's Lana'i photos.

"Oh, you never showed these to me," he said. "They look amazing. May I?" Mark swiped past the beautiful photos of Sienna posing on Shipwreck Beach until he discovered photos of Sienna with a strange man.

"Who's this?" he asked.

Sienna's blood froze. How was she going to explain why she hadn't told him about Tom earlier?

"It's a guy I met while I was touring Lana'i. We ended up hanging out together. His name is Tom."

She explained it matter-of-factly but knew it sounded strange. And she didn't even mention also meeting Tom in La Perouse and again in Hāna.

Mark paled. "You look quite comfortable with each other," he sneered. "Who is this guy? Why were you with him?" His marriage with his ex-wife Isabella had failed because she had cheated on him. He didn't want to go through the same thing with Sienna. His gut churned at the thought.

"I'm sorry, Mark, but he was just a nice guy. Nothing happened. I've been wanting to tell you about him, but there hasn't been a chance."

Mark nodded, not knowing what to think. A wedge grew between them, ruining the relaxed vibe.

"Yeah, sure." Not wanting to say something he'd regret later, he swiped a hand down his face and tossed Sienna's phone back to her. He looked at his watch and curtly said, "I think we should head back now, the park's closing soon."

He started walking without waiting for Sienna. She followed him, her stomach in knots.

Chapter 27

Things weren't the same between Sienna and Mark after Pipiwai Trail. She tried to explain a few times that her relationship with Tom was merely platonic, but Mark didn't want to talk about it. He gave her the cold shoulder and answered monosyllabic every time she said something, until she finally gave up. He sped through the hairpin curves without paying attention to the gorgeous paradise they passed through. When they arrived back at the cottage, Mark climbed out of the Jeep, slammed the door and went to sit by Palila's side without even acknowledging Sienna.

This was a side of Mark Sienna had never experienced. She almost couldn't blame him though. She felt like the lying girlfriend, and her stomach was in knots. She didn't feel like having dinner with the entire family again, so she got in the Jeep and headed into Hāna.

She stopped at the general store. Maybe she'd find some gifts for the kids and grab a sandwich or something simple for dinner. She stepped inside the convenience store that looked like a building in a Western. Dark wood spanned everywhere from the shelves and countertops to the beams in the rustic vaulted ceilings. The shelves were filled with groceries, t-shirts, postcards, books, hats, fishing supplies, over the counter meds, toilet paper and napkins.

Sienna grabbed t-shirts and baseball caps for everyone, some cute picture books for Lilly and Sydney, coffee mugs for the grandparents, and a pretty bracelet for Lindsey. She still needed something for Leo, but maybe she'd make it to Ulupalakua Ranch in Upcountry and find something there.

The sun was setting. Sienna drove around town, but there wasn't anywhere to go or anything to do in the dark. She passed the hotel and decided to stop in for a drink if the bar was open. She walked up to the front desk in the hotel's open-air lobby and asked for directions to the restaurant. To her surprise, Ana's assistant and student, Konani, was working there.

"Yeah, this is my day job. Healing and studying with Ana is my passion. But it doesn't pay the bills."

Sienna understood.

"Well, it was good to see you," Sienna said and continued walking toward the bar. It was mostly empty, but a guitar player in a corner played melancholy Hawaiian tunes.

She sat down, ordered a mai tai and listened to the music, indulging in her sad thoughts. What a vacation this had been! Between Mark's work and staying by him as he dealt with tragedy, she had been isolated and only really enjoyed this paradise sightseeing with Tom. She felt bad but hadn't done anything wrong besides not telling Mark about it.

The door to the bar opened and someone entered. It was Mark. He sighed, relieved to have found Sienna, and made a beeline toward her, taking her in his arms. His lips found hers and they kissed each other passionately. The barkeeper and some of the few guests watched, a bit embarrassed. When the kiss ended, Mark didn't let go of her.

"I'm so sorry about my harsh reaction earlier today. I've been thinking about it. I guess it was unavoidable that you found someone to sightsee and hike with when I was working. It's better you had company than being stranded here alone. I'm sorry I didn't trust you."

"It's okay," replied Sienna. "Tom is a nice guy, but he's seriously just a friend, Mark. You're the one I love. His wife died recently of the same cancer Palila has."

"Wow," said Mark. "That poor guy."

"You need a drink. This has been tough," said Sienna. She turned toward the barkeeper. "Can we please have two more?"

The barkeeper nodded.

"So, how is Palila doing now?" Sienna asked.

"I think it's just a matter of days. I almost feel like I shouldn't be leaving. I have surgery scheduled for Monday morning that I really can't cancel, but I wonder if we should stay here for a few more days. I can just drive back and forth that morning. It's a tough surgery around a honu's eyes and head. I'd hate to leave Billy, the Institute's vet, to do it by himself. It's only a two-hour drive, like going from Turtle Key to Miami and back."

"If you want, I can drive with you for the company," she proposed.

"You might be needed more here with all the kids and everyone being so busy. Have you been able to talk to Nalu more?"

"She's warming up to me, but I'm not sure how things will

change once her mom is gone."

"That's going to be tough for her. You might have to stay longer than a couple more weeks. Maybe I can talk to Richard and Rose about staying a few days longer myself. They do well with the kids."

The barkeeper put the mai tais on the counter in front of them and Mark proposed a toast. "To us, nothing can tear us apart." He kissed her again. "I love you, Sienna, and want to thank you for all your support in the last few days."

She clinked her glass against his and sipped the strong drink. "I love you, Mark, and I'm sorry you—or we—have to go through this. Palila is such a lovely person."

Mark gazed at Sienna, his eyes twinkling.

"By the way, I told Palila that I proposed to you. She seemed pleased with you in the role of stepmom. I hope you're okay with that."

"Yes, she told me she's pleased about that as well." Sienna gave Mark a gentle kiss.

They finished their drinks and walked through the spacious hotel lobby. A water fountain trickled in the middle, surrounded by colorful paintings, including an original Paul Kent.

As they drove back to the house underneath an eerie bright sky with a full moon and scattered clouds, Mark proposed a walk on Hāmoa Beach since neither were tired yet. He parked the Jeep in front of Paul and Luana's. An owl hooted as they walked down the quiet, peaceful road. Branches rustled in the wind, and a cat ran across the street as they walked past Lani and Max's house.

A child yelled, and they realized there was a lot of activity and lights on in the house. Something didn't seem right. They ran up the crunchy gravel driveway.

Max was carefully carrying Palila into the guesthouse and lifted her onto the hospital bed.

"What's going on?" Mark asked, covering Palila with a quilt once they'd laid her on the bed.

"She stayed out by the water longer than usual. She tripped over a root on her way back in the dark and hit the ground hard. Now she's unconscious," said Max.

Nalu was hysterical. "It's my fault! I was supposed to take care of her, and I didn't. It's my fault she's dying!"

Sienna took Nalu in her arms, trying to console her. "Shh, shhh, Nalu. It's okay. It's not your fault. It was an accident."

"I didn't take care of her!"

Sienna pulled her onto the couch and held her tightly, caressing her head as her body convulsed from sobbing.

Luana tried to call Ana and Konani for advice, but neither answered their phones. The only doctor in town was attending a home birth, and Palila had explicitly requested no medical doctors anyhow. Finally, Luana got hold of Ana, but neither Konani nor her granddaughter Pekelo were there to drive her over. Ana hadn't driven in years, so someone had to go and pick her up, a treacherous drive in the dark, even though it was only a few miles.

"I'll go get Ana," Mark volunteered.

"I'll go with you," Sienna said. "Do you want to come, Nalu?"

"No, I need to stay with her." She sniffled and clung to her mother's hand. The situation seemed too grave to leave her side.

The full moon turned out to be a blessing as it provided a bit of light on the dark deserted Hāna Highway. The tall bamboo and tropical plants cast frightening shadows across the road. Mark cursed as he drove down the winding road around the cliffs. Headlights from an oncoming car were visible half a mile ahead, which seemed a blessing at first, but Sienna and Mark were nervous wrecks until the car had passed safely on the narrow road. Mark slammed on the breaks.

"Oh, my gosh!" Sienna gasped. Half a dozen pigs scampered across the road, lit by the bright headlights.

"Of course, they cross now, of all times," Mark said under his breath, wiping the sweat off his forehead.

They finally made it to Ana's house and turned into the overgrown driveway next to a rusty antique car, a landmark showing they had found the right place. Ana was waiting with a thermos of fresh-brewed tea and some other potions in her bag. Sienna helped her climb into the front seat and got in the back.

The drive back seemed even worse, since this time they were on the cliff side of the road, but luckily no cars passed. Ana's calming presence helped Mark concentrate and bring them safely back to Kōkī Beach House. Ana gave Palila some warm tea, supporting her head as she drank, and rubbed some calming eucalyptus essences on her forehead and chest.

"Mama, I'm coming home soon," Palila mumbled. "I'll see you soon." Her eyes never opened as she spoke.

"This is normal," Ana reassured them, though her eyes told

a different story. She waited for Nalu to step out of the guesthouse and said, "It's just a matter of days or even hours now. I don't know if all those visitors should even come tomorrow. It might be too much for her."

The atmosphere was subdued. Mark and Sienna stood side by side with their arms tight around each other. Max shook his head, stroking Lani's back as tears fell silently down her cheeks.

Nalu stood outside the guesthouse door and overheard what Ana said. Her face paled. She silently went back inside, sat down next to her mother's bed and didn't leave her side anymore.

Chapter 28

Palila woke up energetic the next morning, giving Nalu and everyone else a false sense of hope.

"This is normal," Ana explained. "Some people experience a surge of energy days or hours before death." They all waited, fearful of what the new day would bring.

Palila carefully dressed herself, tied her prettiest scarf around her head, and walked down to her favorite spot by the water. She sat down and prepared herself for visitors stopping by today to bid their friend one last farewell. She had not only made a lot of friends in Hāna and the surrounding areas as a surfing instructor, she was also well-known everywhere on the island for her great produce and her beautiful plantation. Her family had provided produce for this side of the island even before Hāna Farms was established.

It was a sad day for Palila's friends, but she joked and pointed at the honu sitting there again and told them not to be sad. "He's waiting for me. I'm going to return as a honu," she told them. In between visits, Nalu sat at her mother's side, holding her hand. Lani had taken the day off, but Luana and Max had to work.

Ana watched over everything. She and Konani provided

fresh tea and pastries all afternoon, making sure Palila took breaks in between and that guests only stayed for so long. It seemed like half the residents of Hāna had been here already. Ana scolded Palila for not resting, but Palila replied, "I want to see my friends now and not when I'm dead."

Coconut Glen brought a big cooler full of his famous vegan ice cream. Laura Cattleya brought one of her paintings. Auntie Charlene came with her daughter Tammy and brought more banana bread from the Ke'anae Peninsula. Lani's grandmother, Tutu Leila, stopped by. She still ran the Island General Store in town even though she was almost eighty years old and getting frail. Her husband Kumu had passed away two years ago. Palila's grandparents had supplied her store with produce fifty years ago, and the families had been friends ever since. Long-lasting relationships connected families everywhere on the island, even during sad times like today. Nobody showed their true feelings, everyone pretended to be happy and upbeat for Palila's sake. It was like a big party.

Mark and Sienna were surprised to see the mood shift at Kōkī Beach House when they came over after lunch. They greeted Coconut Glen who had been announced today's hero. Ice cream was the one thing Palila seemed able to swallow.

Even Josh came to see Palila. He had come on a daytrip to Hāna with his kids. Palila's eyes filled with tears as she saw her old friend approaching through the yard. She got up on her weak legs and walked toward him. They fell into a long embrace. Her and Mark's former partner in crime. There was too much to talk about. Josh sat down with the group around Palila.

The honu, sitting half on the lava rock and half in the water, was watching over the group. Suddenly, Josh who had been looking at him in his thoughts, jumped up and walked a few steps toward him, still keeping the respectful distance of ten feet. He recognized the Turtle Rescue's letters and numbers etched into the side of the honu's carapace and read them.

"Mark, that's our missing honu from Maʻalaea Harbor!"

Mark stood up and stepped next to Josh. They were both ecstatic about Josh's discovery.

"Well, I'll be darned. I wonder how he got all the way to Hāna."

"You never know. Maybe he felt he was needed. But they sure like to travel."

Josh was so happy the honu was found that he immediately texted OʻShen, Nora and Kaipo.

Sienna and Lani walked down to Kōkī Beach with the kids. Sienna was glad she could speak one on one with Lani to tell her that the "Tom issue" had been clarified.

"Well, it wasn't too pleasant. He was taking some pictures with my camera and scrolled through old photos and found some of Tom and me."

"Oh, boy…" replied Lani. "How was his reaction?"

"He was quite mad. I explained that my friendship with Tom is entirely platonic, but his ex-wife cheated on him. I guess you never get over that sort of thing."

"Yeah, I can see that."

"But I guess with this whole situation with Palila and Nalu, he thought about it again and forgave me. He really hasn't paid much attention to me at all. I'm glad I met Tom and had someone to hang out with."

"Tom's a great guy. He was depressed for a while after his wife's death. I'm glad he's doing better now."

A noisy car with a roaring engine sped down the road.

"Kids! Let's walk in the grass until this car passes. He's not being very careful," called Lani. "Traffic can be pretty bad around here," she said to Sienna.

A yellow Corvette blasting its speakers stopped. The driver rolled down the passenger window and leaned over. All color drained from Lani's face.

"Hey, there," said the driver. "Remember me? Joseph McAllen. I didn't get the land behind Hāmoa Beach back then, but I'm working on buying a few properties on the other side of Hāna. And I just bought a former plantation in Wailuku that I'm turning into a spa and hotel. Beautiful place. Come see it when it's done."

He didn't care about waiting for a response or looking out for the children. He just rolled the window back up and stepped on the gas, steering his roaring car past Kōkī Beach and up the hill toward Hāna.

"Oh, no. I have to find out what properties in Hāna he's trying to buy and see what we can all do to fight that as a community." She paused for a second. "Do you think he meant Palila's plantation in Wailuku? That would break my heart."

Sienna wondered if it was Palila's plantation too, and it suddenly dawned on her. Tom had told her he worked for a non-profit organization helping locals with a new law that saved them from paying significant taxes. She had to talk to Mark and Palila about that before Palila was gone.

The kids arrived at the beach and ran ahead, down into the sand.

"Be careful, kids! Don't go into the water, it's too rough."

Sienna and Lani caught up to them, took their slippahs off and stepped into the warm red sand. They loved the feeling of their feet sinking into the soft sand. The trade winds created a beautiful breeze, but the water was wild today. Foam flew through the air as the waves broke and crashed into the sand.

Some daredevil surfers waited for the next wave in the distance. Nalu came up to Sienna and took her hand.

"My mom used to surf here."

"I know, I heard how good she was," Sienna replied. "Maybe one day you can take surfing lessons and become as good as her."

"I don't think anyone can be as good as her," said Nalu wisely, pointing at the surfers getting pummeled by the ocean. "That never happened to her."

———⊶●⊷———

The drive back home to Kihei was long for Josh, Alana and Kimo, but Josh didn't regret coming to Hāna. He was elated he had seen Palila one last time and that they had made up. After Mark left, Palila had avoided Josh. Josh was also elated that the missing honu from Ma'alaea Harbor was accounted for and hadn't been kidnapped.

Josh made a few stops to make the drive more exciting for the kids. He showed them the Shetland pony that always hung out at the Ke'anae Peninsula and stopped at some swimmable waterfalls. But Alana and Kimo were tired and grumpy when he dropped them off. The kids jumped out of the car and ran toward the pretty little cottage on North Kihei Road. Melanie opened the door and hugged both kids. She noticed the Band-Aid on Kimo's knee and immediately started fussing about it.

"Can't you watch out for him?" she scolded Josh. "He always seems to have some new injury when you bring him back."

"He slipped and fell on rocks. No big deal. We cleaned it and put Neosporin on it right away," Josh replied. "It's not so bad, is it, Kimo?" Josh tousled the little boy's hair.

"It hurts a little. But we saw some honu and rescued one with Dad yesterday!"

Melanie perked her ears up and Josh got ready for the next blow. "Oh, you're taking the kids to work now too? Next time please call me, and I'll come pick them up if you have a work emergency."

"It's interesting for the kids, Mel."

"Well, I don't like them hanging out at the turtle hospital. There's too many germs. And what if a turtle bites them?"

Josh didn't know what to say about so much ridiculousness. He lifted his hands and let them drop to his sides.

"We drove all the way to Hāna today, Mom. We're tired now."

Melanie gave him another dirty look and said, "When you take the kids on such a dangerous drive, I'd like to know."

Josh defended himself. "It was fine, and we had fun. Didn't

we have fun, kids?"

They nodded.

"Okay, well thanks. I get to deal with my tired grumpy kids for the rest of the day," Melanie said.

Josh ignored her.

"See you next week, kids!" he said.

The kids were already lying on the floor playing with the dog Melanie's boyfriend had gotten them and just yelled, "Bye Dad!"

Josh moped back to his car and drove to his house in Wailea. He hated dropping off the kids and not seeing them again for another week, but at least he had the function tonight.

───────※───────

Just as Josh had almost arrived at the house in Wailea, he received a phone call from Nora.

"I wanted to let you know that Ryan has been talking to his boss about the planned honu purchase at Ma'alaea Harbor tomorrow. He wants me to join him to check if the honu he's buying is healthy… It's scheduled for 7 am."

"Thanks, Nora. I'll let O'Shen know. I guess I'll see you later at the function?"

Nora had also informed him that she was attending the function at Mama's Fish House with Julian Jensen and his entourage.

Chapter 29

Mama's Fish House had been decked out for the annual Visitors & Convention Bureau's fundraiser, held a week before Thanksgiving. Twinkling lights hung everywhere, strands of flowers and leis dangled from the building and the trees. Since the inside of the restaurant wasn't big enough for the many guests, additional tables had been set up on the lawn in front of the restaurant all the way down to the ocean. Colorful flower arrangements decorated each table. Guests walked down the stairs from the host stand on a red carpet and were greeted as their pictures were taken by the local press.

Everyone who worked closely with the Convention Bureau and brought the most tourists to Maui had been invited. Popular tours, helicopter flights and upscale hotel stays were being auctioned off. The proceeds went to a charity to be announced that evening.

Josh usually despised such formal events and hated small talk even more, but he wanted to do O'Shen a favor and loved Mama's food so much that he would endure a stiff evening. He was also glad to have a distraction after his last unpleasant encounter with his ex-wife. He planned on being a frequent visitor to the open bar tonight and taking an uber home. Feeling uncomfortable in his black suit, tie and dress shoes he only got out of the closet maybe once a year, Josh waited in front of the host stand until O'Shen arrived. He tugged at his tie to loosen it and turned toward the parking lot, stunned as O'Shen walked up to him.

Her athletic body, courtesy of the marathons she ran on a regular basis, had been squeezed into a tight black floor-length sheath dress. Her long jet-black hair with some strands of white was pulled up into an elegant knot and covered by a colorful haku lei. A black evening purse and matching pumps completed her simple yet elegant style. Josh took her arm, they checked in at the host stand and walked down the red carpet.

"Thanks for coming. I hate this kind of formal event myself," O'Shen said. "Let's go and get a drink at the bar first so we can stand it."

"I'm right behind you."

They scanned the room from the bar. Executives of the biggest hotels and everyone with rank and name on the island of Maui was here along with celebrities invited to bid generously on the auction. TV station owner, producer, actor and hotelier Julian Jensen from Lana'i was here with Nora, her "friend" Ryan and an entire entourage at a prime table.

Josh said quietly to O'Shen, "Over there, at Julian Jensen's table, do you see Nora? She called me earlier and confirmed that the honu purchase tomorrow is still on for 7 am."

O'Shen nodded slyly and took a closer look.

"The guy next to her friend Ryan, looks like the guy Steve that my undercover cop Jon Jon talked to the other day. I can't wait to hear what else she picks up from their conversation."

Josh looked briefly at Nora one more time, then he followed O'Shen to their assigned table.

O'Shen and Josh sat down at the "police" table, joining some of O'Shen's bosses and coworkers. O'Shen's assistant Christine had managed to get an invitation and was there with her husband Koa, a kanaka who volunteered for the Turtle Rescue.

"So, what's the status on the honu?" he asked Josh and O'Shen.

"We have a few leads but can't talk about them yet," said O'Shen. She looked at Christine. It must be hard not to discuss these things with her husband, but she knew she could trust Christine.

"Lots of locals are very concerned," Koa replied. "The honu are an important part of our culture. We don't understand how someone could take or harm them."

O'Shen nodded. "We are watching the beaches around the clock as are the neighborhood watches. So far, we have no proof that any honu were taken."

A row of waiters walked up with their main courses, interrupting their conversation. They set the plates down and wished everyone "E hau'oli i kāu'ai"—bon appetit in Hawaiian. Everyone oohed and aahed. It was opakapaka: pink snapper with soy sauce, caramelized onions, shiitake mushrooms, green onions with ginger and a side of basmati rice.

All conversations stopped as the guests enjoyed their main course. Following the fish, Mama's signature black pearl dessert, a chocolate mousse with a lilikoi center, draped in chocolate ganache and served with toasted coconut whipped cream and a pastry seashell, was served.

Only some heartfelt comments about the "ono grindz" and "broke da mouth" interrupted the silence.

After dinner, the auction began. For Josh, the boring part of the evening. He was ready to go home but walked over to the bar for a drink instead. He ran into Nora as he passed the restrooms. She sparkled in a black sequined dress. Her matching heels made her taller than usual. She looked like a young Annie Lennox with her short platinum blonde hair and her chiseled jawline.

She glanced around nervously and said, "I guess we should act surprised to be running into each other?"

"Yes," he replied quietly. He wasn't a very good actor but said loudly, "Oh, hey Nora! What are you doing here?"

"Oh, I'm just hanging out with some friends of mine," she said vaguely and smiled.

"Well, I was about to leave. It was good to see you. I'll see you tomorrow morning, I guess."

"Yes," she said and walked back to her table. Ryan looked at her and asked: "Was that your boss? What did he want?"

"Oh, he was just surprised to see me here and told me how hard it was to get tickets for tonight."

Ryan whispered into Jensen's ear and they both laughed heartily. "Not for us, hahaha!"

Jensen looked over at O'Shen, Josh and the police table but just continued laughing as he bid on another high-priced item. Nothing and nobody could intimidate him, not even the table full of local police officers.

Chapter 30

Apiercing wail went through the guesthouse, heard all the way over in Kōkī Beach House, maybe even in Hāna. When Nalu woke up and checked on her mother, Palila's soul had departed her body. Nalu gently shook her. "Mama. Mama! Wake up!" But she couldn't answer anymore. Palila was gone.

Ana, who had a cot set up in the corner of the room to keep a close eye on Palila, jerked awake and shuffled over to check Palila's pulse. Palila had used all her strength to entertain her friends yesterday, but her weakened body had finally given up.

"I'm sorry, Nalu, your mom is gone," she said gently. "She is in a better place now, in no more pain anymore. She's gone on to paradise. She suffered a lot but didn't show us. She was a strong woman, your mama."

She took Nalu in her arms, but Nalu wouldn't calm down. She thrashed until she freed herself, throwing herself onto Palila's bed. "Mama! Please come back!" she cried.

Ana laid a hand on Nalu's shoulder. "I'm so sorry," she said again. Nalu stormed out of the guesthouse and ran down to the water, her mother's last favorite place. Nalu checked if her mom's friend, the honu, was there. He was gone too, just like her mother. She sobbed next to the water.

Ana walked over to the main house to let Lani and her family know what had happened. They called Mark, Sienna, Paul and Luana. Everyone came over to gather around Palila. Even though they had prepared and knew she was in a better place now, everyone cried. Mark called and cancelled the surgery he was supposed to perform later today.

Sienna looked around and realized Nalu was missing. "Has anyone seen Nalu?"

"I think she went down to Palila's favorite spot down by the ocean," replied Ana.

Sienna and Mark walked down to the water, looking for Nalu, but she wasn't there. They checked in Nalu's bed, the bathroom, in Kai and Paulo's rooms, the entire Kōkī Beach House. They even checked the garage and the laundry room in front of the guesthouse. But she was nowhere to be found. Everyone was worried since the road could be very dangerous with all the tourists and speeders.

Sienna checked the guesthouse one more time, just in case. No Nalu. She sat heavily in the armchair Palila had rested in down by the water. This wasn't the only place that Palila had favored. Two more spots had given her peace: Kōkī Beach and Hāmoa Beach, where she had meditated and transported herself onto a surfboard again. Something that made her feel happy and peaceful. Palila had talked to Nalu about it many times and encouraged her to learn the five-minute meditation that Ana had taught her.

Sienna told Mark, and they decided that he'd go to Kōkī Beach, and she'd go to Hāmoa Beach. Sienna hurried the few hundred feet down to Hāmoa Beach. She passed the outlook under the big wooded plumeria, the bench, which looked like a deserted bus stop, then she headed down the stairs. The beach was still vacant this early in the morning. Sienna walked to the left where she and Mark liked to set up camp at the foot of the rocks under the shady trees. But Nalu wasn't there.

Sienna turned around and walked all the way to the other end of the beach that was also shaded by trees and ended in a steep hill and an overgrown emergency entrance. There Nalu was. She had climbed onto a rock overlooking the ocean and sat with her eyes closed, her face lifted to the sky. Sienna texted Mark that she had found Nalu. Then she climbed up the rock and sat down next to her. They sat quietly next to each other for a while, listening to the waves crashing on the beach. The sun still hadn't come out, making the air chilly. Finally, Nalu stirred, coming out of her meditation. She inhaled and exhaled deeply, then blinked a few times and opened her eyes.

To Sienna's surprise, Nalu smiled. "I just went surfing with my mom." It didn't bring her mom back, but it gave her a tiny bit of peace. Sienna smiled with tears in her eyes and took her in her arms as they gazed out at the ocean.

After receiving Sienna's text message, Mark informed everyone Nalu had been found. He sat down next to Palila. His tears flowed freely as he bid farewell to his old friend, teacher and first love and remembered the carefree days of young adulthood.

FLASHBACK # 1

approx. 11 years ago @ Hāmoa Beach

Mark and Palila ran down the beach with their surfboards. They treaded past the wave break, threw their surfboards down, and paddled into deeper waters. On Palila's command, they turned their surfboards around and waited for the next promising wave. Mark watched every move Palila made. Palila knew it and pointed at things he should pay attention to.

She signaled to start paddling and yelled, "Go!" They paddled with all their might until they felt the wave. They crouched on the boards and catapulted forward, gliding across the ocean's surface. Adrenaline coursed through Mark's body. Palila waved as she ducked out of sight. Mark searched for her and discovered her zigzagging across the waves far ahead. Not paying enough attention to himself, he wiped out and flew into the strong whitewater, his surfboard flying around his head. He came up gasping for air, grabbed his surfboard tethered to his ankle and let the waves wash him ashore.

Palila was already waiting. They could've continued for hours, but it was getting dark and cooling off. They were the last people on the beach. The sun went down behind the hills, the sky glowing pink and red.

FLASHBACK # 2

approx. 11 years ago @ Waianapanapa State Park

Palila and Mark sat in front of their tent, arguing about Mark applying for a job in Florida. He was departing tomorrow for an interview in the Keys.

Palila, her face beet red in anger, yelled at Mark, "So, this past year meant nothing to you? What about us?"

"What will I do for the rest of my life?" he yelled. "Sell produce? What was the point of the last eight years of college if I stay to do that?"

Palila flinched as if he'd slapped her. She was proud of her family's plantation and selling produce for several generations.

She mumbled, "I thought you loved me," grabbed her backpack, got in the car and left him stranded. She never spoke to him again.

BACK TO PRESENT TIME

Kōkī Beach House – Guesthouse

Mark wept. He was shocked how much he still loved Palila. She had been stubborn, bossy and bull-headed, but she would always be a part of him, especially now that Nalu was in the picture.

———◦———

After sitting at the beach all morning, Sienna and Nalu walked back to Kōkī Beach House along pretty beach cottages surrounded by tropical foliage.

Nalu asked, "Do you think I could come and visit you guys in Florida? I'd like to meet my half-sister."

"You kind of have four half-sisters and brothers," noted Sienna, "we're all one big family. I have three kids too that I adopted."

"How did you adopt them?"

"My sister and brother-in-law, the kids' parents, died in a car accident and there was no one besides me to take care of them."

Nalu thought about that for a while. So, she wasn't the only kid whose parent had died.

"Did they get over it?"

"I don't think you ever get over it. Time helps a little, then you have your happy memories but also your sad moments."

Nalu nodded.

"How old are they?"

"Lilly is seven, Lindsey is fourteen, Leo is seventeen. And Sydney is seven as well. Lilly and Sydney are in the same class. You'd love them all. We take the boat out often on the weekends and go snorkeling. There's no or hardly any surfing in the Keys though. The waves aren't big enough."

Nalu looked at Sienna and then at the wild ocean. *Ouch,* thought Sienna. *That could be a deal breaker.* But she had to tell Nalu the truth.

"I guess I could come here on vacation, right?"

"I'd like all of us to go," replied Sienna. "But it's a long flight."

"But I have to stay here and wait for my mom to come as a honu and visit me. She won't be able to swim all the way to Florida."

They arrived at Kōkī Beach House and took a right into the guesthouse. Mark was sitting by himself next to Palila. With the shades still closed, the room was dark. Nothing had been changed since they had found Palila this morning. Sienna hugged Mark. With tears in his eyes, he held Sienna tightly. She hated seeing him so sad. All three of them sat there crying about Palila as Ana stepped in.

She said, "It's okay to cry, guys. By releasing and expressing the 'eha, the sorrow, the ohana and friends can deal with loss in a healthier way, and the kau, the burden of sorrow, is lifted faster."

Lani entered with a big plate of pancakes. Despite their grief, they all helped themselves and ate.

Chapter 31

Right before sunrise, undercover agent Jon Jon was prepared to go over to Ma'alaea Harbor and sell a honu to Steve and his boss Ryan in a sting operation.

Undercover cops worked in the harbor, getting boats ready to go out fishing or on tours, or hid and watched what was going on. The harbor hustled and bustled with everyone preparing for the upcoming day on the island where the water hosted all the most important activities: fishing, diving, snorkeling, whale watching and cruises.

Ma'alaea, one of the most central spots on Maui, was also one of the windiest. The northeasterly trade winds blew over the West Maui Mountains into the valley of Wa'alaea which acted as a giant wind tunnel and caused wind speeds of up to forty miles per hour.

The U-shaped harbor and manmade seawall protected the boats from bigger swells due to the strong winds. O'Shen's crew was lucky that the "Lana'i Princess" was in an odd slip, #27. Odd-numbered slips were all on the land side, evens on the ocean side. The officers hid behind buildings along the harbor rather than in the open. O'Shen wondered if the dockmaster had made an exception for the yacht; The "Lana'i

Princess" seemed to exceed the usual size allowed to anchor in the harbor. The dockmaster had been accused of shady business practices and accepting bribes in the past, and O'Shen kept a special eye on him. She made a note to check if the yacht fit the harbor regulations.

The "Lana'i Princess" was a 120-foot-long yacht with a helipad, registered to Julian Jensen. Of course this made sense, but it seemed too predictable. Would Jensen really be this dumb and do something like this after announcing it on TV?

Josh's presence had been forbidden during this morning's mission, but he snuck down to the harbor nonetheless and hid in a safe spot. He had volunteered one of the honu from the Maui Turtle Rescue that lived long-term in captivity due to a damaged carapace. She was used to being handled on a regular basis, but Josh wanted to make sure that Jenny was safe and handled properly.

Jenny had been covered with a sheet in a large plastic bin that Jon Jon was now pushing down the dock on a dolly. He stopped at the glitzy three-story yacht. Ryan strutted down the gangway in his designer clothes and aviator sunglasses, followed by Steve, another assistant and Nora. She was a bit nervous and walked a bit too slow, but Ryan took her hand, pulling her up to the honu in the container.

Nora pretended to examine Jenny to ascertain her health and nodded. Suddenly, Ryan pushed Nora aside brusquely and took a closer look. Not only did the honu have a tattoo etched in her carapace, the honu's carapace also looked like it had some old significant damage to it. He stared at Nora who started sweating and hissed at her angrily, "You're telling me that this honu is okay?"

Nora panicked and tried to run away, but Ryan held her arm and yelled, "This is a set up!" He ran back onto the yacht, pulling Nora along as a hostage.

Jon Jon pulled out a gun, pointed it at Steve and the other assistant before they could run away and yelled, "Stop and put your hands up!" Two other undercover agents ran up and pointed their guns at the honu dealers, leaving Jon Jon free to follow Ryan who was holding his gun up to Nora as he pulled her along. Nobody had expected Nora to get in such life-threatening danger, and everyone was quite shocked.

Several other police officers, including O'Shen, ran up from all sides and followed Jon Jon onto the yacht. Josh ran up to pull Jenny in safety. Jon Jon ran through the yacht and down a staircase leading below deck. He passed down a long hallway, ignoring the rooms with open doors, and skidded to a stop at the locked state room on the far end. As he jiggled the door handle, O'Shen caught up with him.

Jon Jon rammed the door with his shoulder, and it burst open. They held their guns in position and inched into the master state room with a king size bed. Another door leading to a bathroom was also locked. They couldn't hear anything and broke that door open as well, and there was Nora, still shaking in shock. As soon as Ryan had realized that his only chance for escape was climbing through a very small porthole, he changed his mind about taking Nora as a hostage. He pushed her into a corner and jumped out of the window instead, diving into the harbor water.

Nora sat crouched in the corner, crying. O'Shen kneeled

down next to her, making sure she was unharmed.

"Search the water and the entire area for that jerk," yelled O'Shen. "He got away!"

The police feverishly searched the water and the entire harbor, looking for Ryan, but he was nowhere to be found.

"We have to get him before he's able to warn Jensen!" shouted O'Shen. She noticed the helicopter on the helipad. "Can anyone here fly this thing?" she yelled.

None of the police officers reacted, but an old rugged-looking local fisherman who had stood by watching the whole situation raised his hand. "I flew one in 'Nam. And I work with one of the local helicopter companies flying tourists from time to time. This one might be a bit more complicated, but I can probably figure it out."

"Let's go," yelled O'Shen and ran up to the helicopter. "Jon Jon, Christine, come on!"

She asked the older fisherman, "What's your name?" as she climbed inside and put on one of the headsets hanging in the cockpit.

"Kurt," he replied as he climbed into the pilot's seat and started switching buttons on.

"Thanks for volunteering, Kurt," O'Shen replied as she nodded at him, full of respect. "And thanks for your service in Vietnam. My name is O'Shen, and this is Jon Jon and Christine."

"Aloha kakahiaka, guys."

Jon Jon and Christine had reluctantly followed O'Shen and climbed into the helicopter. They didn't feel comfortable flying with this guy who only flew "from time to time," but they didn't have a choice when O'Shen had her mind set on something. And it was a time sensitive matter.

———————◦———————

The sun coming up behind the cliffs of Lana'i blinded the pilot and passengers as the Eurocopter Hermes EC 135 moved closer to the island. O'Shen handed Kurt her sunglasses without comment. Kurt had quickly figured out how to fly this brand-new luxury helicopter. The GPS took them straight to the last destination, Julian Jensen's estate in southwest Lana'i, just a few miles away from one of the luxurious resorts he owned.

Jensen's monstrous two-story mansion behind a private beach could already be seen from afar.

As the helicopter touched down on the helipad, everything was quiet on the property, it almost seemed deserted. O'Shen, her two colleagues and Kurt climbed out of the helicopter, the police officers pulling out their guns, carefully assessing the situation. They walked down to the dock, but nobody was there. Then they walked to the front door of the impressive mansion and knocked. A butler dressed in a vest, grey trousers, a white shirt and a black tie opened the door.

"May I help you, ladies and gentlemen?" he asked in perfect Oxford English.

"We'd like to talk to Mr. Jensen, please," replied O'Shen, looking quizzically at her colleagues.

"Please, step in," replied the butler well-mannered. "I'll let Mr. Jensen know you're here. Do you happen to have a business card?"

O'Shen replied abruptly. "No, just tell him the Maui police is here. We don't have time for these shenanigans."

The butler replied without blinking, "Please follow me," and led them through a giant foyer with a fancy staircase leading to the second floor. They noticed an electric stairlift on the side of the stairs as used by handicapped people. They continued through several formal living-rooms and a library to a big sunroom full of orchids where Julian Jensen, wearing an elegant bathrobe with a crest on its chest, was sitting in an armchair, reading a newspaper.

"Mr. Jensen, the Maui police are here to speak with you. I'm sorry I couldn't give you proper notice, but they seem pressed for time."

Jensen took his time, neatly folded his newspaper without even looking up and set it down on a table next to his armchair.

"Good morning, ladies and gentlemen. Can I offer you coffee or anything else to drink? I grow my own coffee beans on property, you might appreciate that."

"Mr. Jensen, we'd like to know what's going on here. Three of your assistants were just caught red-handed trying to buy a honu at your yacht in Ma'alaea Harbor," said O'Shen. "As you know that is an extraordinary criminal offense. Honu are sacred, and protected by several laws."

Without even blinking, Jensen replied: "Ma'am, I have no idea what you're talking about. I've been here in my residence all morning, having my MS treatments, which my physical therapists can confirm." He slowly grabbed an antique looking cane with a golden handle and stood up in a laborious manner. He was tall and lanky, most of his muscle mass had obviously disappeared due to his illness, he held up one of his shaky hands as to prove how disabled he was.

"Do I really look like a honu dealer to you?" Assisted by his cane, he limped over to one of his beautiful orchids and smelled it. "This Cattleya really has the most beautiful scent in the morning. Would you like to smell it?"

O'Shen and her colleagues were flabbergasted. Obviously, they were being fooled or Jensen had, indeed, nothing to do with the attempted honu purchase at Ma'alaea Harbor.

"I might have said that I could afford to buy a honu as my personal "aumakua" on TV, but do you really think I'd be so disrespectful to the Hawaiian culture to do that? If I gave you or anyone else the impression, I apologize. I'm on borrowed time. I certainly wouldn't want to upset any of the gods that may decide about my afterlife."

He sounded sincere, and they had no proof that he had been involved.

"Do you know where your assistants are right now, Mr. Jensen?" asked O'Shen? "And are you aware that they were using your yacht in Ma'alaea Harbor for this attempted honu purchase?"

Jensen shook his head. "No. But trust me, they won't be coming here. Or if they do, I'll let you know. I do not support any of this, and they're fired as of right now. As for them using my yacht, I'll make sure that they don't have access to it in the future. Now, if you'll excuse me, I have my next treatment in my gym. For any other questions you can speak with my lawyers..."

He limped out of the room and just left them there.

O'Shen's nostrils were flaring. Even if Jensen had anything to do with this, there was nothing she could do to prove it. She had to catch Ryan and start interrogating the other two assistants.

Since they were at a dead-end right now, and the helicopter's range wasn't big enough to fly back, O'Shen, her colleagues and Kurt the pilot walked down to the beach, waiting for the Coast Guard to take them back to Maui.

"What about Ryan?" asked O'Shen the Coast Guard colleagues. "Has he been caught yet?"

"No, we're still looking."

O'Shen sent units to the airport, Lahaina Harbor and even to Molokai, but Ryan wasn't found.

Chapter 32

Mark mourned Palila. He was even more absent than he had been during the past week, but Sienna let him be. She understood. Though he hadn't seen Palila in more than ten years, this was a tough blow. In the afternoon, Sienna decided they should all go to the beach to get out of the dark guesthouse. She sent Nalu over to the main house to ask if anyone wanted to join them. Lani packed a picnic basket, and she and the kids joined Mark, Sienna and Nalu. Even Ana came, she needed a break from sadness too.

They all walked down to the beach like ducks in a row, keeping a slow pace to accommodate Ana who walked with her cane. The last week had exhausted her, and it showed. Clouds covered the sun, casting a gray gloom over the ocean, but some frolicking visitors weren't letting the weather ruin their enthusiasm.

Great frigatebirds zoomed back and forth, letting the wind carry them across the sky. Kai and Paolo played with their boogie boards in the shallow water before the first wave break. Nalu walked back over to her meditation spot on the lava rock with a hanging head. Even the beautiful beach couldn't cheer her up today. She sat looking at the ocean.

Mark joined her.

"Did you love my mom?" asked Nalu.

"Yes, I did."

"How come you have another daughter? What's her name? Sydney?"

"Well, it was a different life in Florida. People move on. Your mom would have never come to Florida, and I couldn't stay alone for the rest of my life."

"So, I'll have to move on and get a new mom, so I don't have to stay alone the rest of my life? How can I do that? Wouldn't I forget about my mom?" she asked with tears in her eyes.

"You won't forget about her. You just learn to love more people. You can love more than one. You'll always have your memories of her, just like I will." Mark put his arm around her.

It didn't make Nalu feel better. Right now, she was certain she'd be betraying her mom if she went to Florida with Sienna and Mark.

"Your mom would want you to be happy. Not lonely and sad," added Mark.

Mark wasn't sure he'd be able to take Nalu to Florida. They might have a long road ahead of them until she was ready.

The sun hid behind the clouds, and the trade winds blew a cool breeze, so everyone napped peacefully on their towels after playing in the water.

Max showed up after work and brought two surfboards. Everyone cheered. The waves weren't strong today, good for beginners.

"Okay, guys, who's first?" asked Max. "How about you,

Nalu? I bet you inherited your mom's talent."

At first, she didn't want to, but then she reluctantly went with Max.

"You've surfed with your mom before, haven't you?" he asked as they walked toward the water. "I don't have to show you all that beginner stuff like how to paddle and such, do I?"

"No, I can even stand sometimes," she said proudly, warming up to Max's happy-go-lucky nature.

He made sure her surfboard's tether was fastened to her ankle and said, "Okay, let's go then, hāele pū!"

They stepped into the chilly water and threw the surfboards ahead of them, pushing them deeper and deeper as they leaped chest first on top of the boards. Max was surprised how strong Nalu's paddle strokes were. They were out in deeper water in no time.

They lay on their surfboards, waiting for the perfect wave. Max signaled Nalu to paddle. They paddled as hard as they could, and Nalu jumped up, riding the wave like a pro! She rode the wave all the way to shore, Max next to her. Sienna, Mark and the kids cheered her on.

"Great job!"

"Wow, you're already nearly as good as your mom," said Max, laughing happily. "I'm impressed. Wanna try again?"

Nalu did, but then she saw Kai's face.

"No, Kai can have a turn," she said.

"Mahalo, Nalu," said Kai, giving her a hug.

Kai paddled into deeper water with her dad. Sienna, Mark and Nalu walked back up to Lani's picnic.

———————◦———————

Everyone had left the beach except Mark, Sienna, Ana and Nalu who had fallen asleep again. Mourning robbed her energy, and she had slept a lot today. Ana said it was good for healing, so they waited and didn't wake her up.

Night fell and the moon rose high in the sky. Before they left, they walked up to the lava rocks and sat down quietly, listening to the waves.

Drumming came from the hills and then music, like an orchestra playing. Sienna raised a questioning eyebrow at Mark. Nalu hid her face in Sienna's arms.

Ana held her finger up to her mouth, motioning everyone to stay quiet. She whispered, "Don't look straight into their eyes. It's huaka'i pō, the night marchers. According to legend, the night marchers are ancient Hawaiian warriors. Today, their spirits roam different areas on the islands, some of them former battlefields. They look like ghostly spirits, carrying torches and playing drums as they chant. They are most active at night but have also been seen during the day. Nothing stops their path; they can walk right through walls or hills.

"If you come across the night marchers, you're not supposed to interrupt them. You should also never look at them directly, or their deadly glance could kill you. If you see these spirits, remain silent, with your eyes looking down. Always show them the respect they deserve."

She stopped talking and let the procession pass, looking down respectfully. Sienna and Nalu were so scared they closed their eyes.

Ana continued explaining, "I've heard about them but never saw them this clearly. I wonder if this has something to do with Palila's death. She told me once that many of her ancestors were warriors."

Chills ran down Sienna's spine. This had been a truly scary but humbling experience. They had all really felt the presence of the warriors.

Ana said, "Some souls don't leave Earth. They are wandering spirits, or *laper,* and the living fear them."

They sat for a while, shocked about what they had just seen. Was it real or just a phenomenon? It was too much of a coincidence that they had all seen the same thing.

"It's an honor to see them, and I'm sure it has to do with your mother's death. Maybe they came to see her," Ana said to Nalu.

As they left, Nalu walked close to Sienna and whispered, "I don't know if I can ever come here again in the dark."

"I think I agree with you," said Sienna, grabbing Mark's arm and walking a bit closer to him. Nalu, Sienna and Mark were all huddled close, as if to protect each other. And it felt good even to Nalu.

They gathered their belongings and walked back to Kōkī Beach House, silent in their thoughts.

The moon hid behind some clouds, Venus and the first stars of the night appeared in the sky.

Chapter 33

The next day, Mark drove back to the Maui Turtle Rescue to perform laser surgery on the honu that had FP on his head and around his eyes. Veterinarian Billy assisted him. Sienna decided to join him and asked Nalu if she wanted to come. She tried to persuade her by mentioning the dogs Arnold Palmer and Ben Hogan.

They needed to get Nalu out of the guesthouse. The funeral home had come to take her mom away to be cremated. Nalu hadn't handled the situation well when she found out her mom was gone. She wanted to stay in the guesthouse by herself but couldn't. Ana volunteered to stay with her, but she was too tired and exhausted. Everyone agreed she had to go home and rest. Nalu would have to move over to the main house. They were all too worried about her.

Palila's ashes were going to be returned to them in a few days, and the ceremony at Hāmoa Beach was scheduled for the following weekend when most friends were available. Sienna postponed her flight back to Florida until the following Sunday. Mark still had to take care of emptying and selling the motorhome.

"You might have to help me sort through things in case

there are some memories of your mom in the motorhome that you want to keep," said Mark to Nalu.

Nalu remembered her mom's small orchid collection behind the trailer that had been fending for itself out in the rain. Too much rain wasn't good for orchids because it rotted their roots. Her mom had brought her two favorite orchids to Kōkī Beach House, but there were at least ten more that had to be rescued.

She nodded. "I'll come."

Saying goodbye to Lani and her family as well as Ana and Pekelo was tough after what they had all experienced together. But they'd be back in a few days, and it felt good to leave the sadness behind and move forward.

Mark, Sienna and Nalu packed the Jeep, gave everyone a hug goodbye and started the trip back to Kihei. Nalu took her mom's two orchids. Lani had offered to keep them in her greenhouses, but Nalu was determined to care for them.

Since it was about the same distance, they continued driving forward and took the back road so Sienna could see the beautiful views and go to Ulupalakua Ranch Store for more gifts.

The road from Hāmoa Beach to Haleakalā Visitor Center was the hairiest part of the Hāna Highway with sometimes only a one lane road winding along the cliffs and steep hills. Used to the drive, Nalu read a book, catching up on some homework. Sienna held onto the handle above her door for dear life.

"Please slow down, Mark! How do you know that no one's

coming behind this curve?" she shouted as a big SUV approached in the curve. Since the SUV had a tiny shoulder on the side, he stopped and let Mark pass first. Mark had nowhere to back up to with the steep cliff on his passenger side just a few inches away.

After passing through the lush jungle of Kipahulu, the curvy muddy road descended to sea level and passed a rocky beach lined with tall coconut palms. A white concrete bridge crossed a stream coming out of the mountains. Its name, Alelele Bridge, had been stamped on it when it was built in the early 1900s. Lush awapuhi ginger, maunaloa flowers and apple trees filled the mountainside.

"My mom and I used to hike up those trails with Ana and collect the ginger that you can wash your hair with. I think it's called awapuhi," Nalu murmured. She leaned her head against the window, watching the scenery pass, lost in her memories. Sienna reached back and put her hand on Nalu's knee in a sympathetic manner.

A few miles after passing the Kaupo store, they stopped at St. Joseph's Church so Sienna could take some pictures. There was already a Christmas wreath on the gate. Mark opened it, and they walked down toward the ocean. The church was closed and had fallen into disrepair. A couple sat in the grass. The man was painting, and the woman was his model. A beautiful sight.

"That seems to be how Paul and Luana met. What a great story," said Sienna.

"Have you ever been here, Nalu?" asked Mark.

"We've driven by but never stopped here. We were mostly

working and delivering fruits and vegetables and wanted to get back home by dark."

Nalu had tears in her eyes, thinking about the fun she and her mom had on their excursions together.

After Kaupo, the terrain dramatically changed. It became sparse and rough, with gorges and canyons leading up the hills of Haleakalā and steep cliffs on the oceanside. Mark slowed down to cross a rattling cattle guard then stopped and waited for an entire herd of cows to cross the road.

Countless windmills dotted the hilly oceanside with gorgeous views of Molokini, Kaho'olawe and Lana'i in the distance.

The road became better, having been recently paved, but it was hilly and felt like a rollercoaster ride. Nalu enjoyed the ride, Sienna not so much. They arrived upcountry at the Ulupalakua Ranch Store and stopped for burgers and refreshments. Sienna was happy to find more great gifts and a sweatshirt for Leo.

It felt good to get out and do some sightseeing after the past few sad days in Hāna. They were excited to see Josh, Arnold Palmer and Ben Hogan when they arrived at the house in Wailea, but they were also tired. Arnold Palmer and Ben Hogan were elated to see Nalu. They were good for her. Nothing helped cure sadness better than two golden retrievers licking your face.

Josh had some good news for them. "Ryan, Jensen's assistant, was caught at Kahului airport trying to leave the island with a fake ID," he reported over dinner.

"What's going to be his and his two assistants'

punishment?" asked Mark.

"I'm not sure yet. They're all awaiting trial and being kept in custody because they're a flight risk. Thank goodness, no honu was actually kidnapped, due to O'Shen's department's help and the diligent work of the neighborhood watches. But they will still be facing possible jail time and high fines. And now listen to this: Jensen donated a significant amount to the turtle rescue and has apologized on TV about what he said and has also distanced himself from what Ryan and his other assistants did. He says he had no idea, and even if they were trying to do this for him as a favor, he is horrified that anyone would have hired someone to catch a honu. Whether that's the truth and the people of Maui and Lana'i will forgive him or not, I do believe he's a sick man trying to make amends. I like to believe in the good in people."

Later, Josh told Mark, "I'm going out on a date with my neighbor Anne tomorrow. We ran into each other this morning while I was walking the dogs and realized we have a ton in common. She went to veterinary school but then had kids and supported her husband in his practice. Now she's divorced. Seems very nice."

"I'm happy for you, brah." Mark grinned and patted Josh's shoulder.

Chapter 34

Nalu, hurry up, we're meeting Mark in twenty minutes," said Sienna, knocking at Nalu's door. She and Nalu wanted to help Mark work in the trailer. Mark called to inform her that he was heading over since he was done with all his surgeries for the day. Nalu had been busy making up missed schoolwork. Sienna caught up with work for the Boston law firm she'd procrastinated on all morning after taking the dogs for a long walk. They were getting along well so far and seemed to be settling into some sort of routine.

Sienna thought Nalu was in her room getting ready. When there was no answer, she opened the door to an empty room. Sienna checked the bathroom and called Nalu again. For a moment, she panicked. She hoped Nalu hadn't run away again. She had no idea where to search for her in Wailea. She looked upstairs, downstairs and then ran out into the garden.

Followed by the two golden retrievers, Nalu had dragged a rusty old metal shelf from the garage to a corner in the backyard and placed her mom's two orchids on it. It barely supported the two pots without falling over, it was so dilapidated. She looked at her work with tears in her eyes. As Sienna walked up, she said, "There are some more orchids at the trailer that I have to rescue." She cried harder.

"Why didn't you ask me to help you, sweetheart?" Sienna took her in her arms. "Maybe we can go to a gardening shop and buy a table or better shelf. And guess what, if you come to Florida, I have a collection of orchids that we can add these to."

Sienna knew shipping them to Florida would be a problem with the Department of Agriculture, but she could worry about that later.

Nalu smiled at her. "Mahalo."

Mark was already at the motorhome talking to the guys at the produce stand. He hadn't even thought about Palila's rented space or that she provided all the produce for the stand. The workers hadn't sold any produce for the past week since they had no supplier. And Palila hadn't paid the two men for the last week they worked. They were Palila's friends and understood the situation, but they had to pay their bills and feed their families as well.

"We get it, but we need our money, brah."

"We'll figure something out. Mahalo, guys. Please write down how much Palila owes you. We're going to have to sell this motorhome, and I can pay you from that money."

They nodded.

"Also, do you know who rented this spot to Palila? I need to cancel it or find someone else who can take over," Mark added.

"I think she rented the spot from some lady at Maui County," replied one of the guys.

"Okay, she must have some paperwork or rental agreement in the trailer. I'll try to find it. Thanks, guys."

Sienna and Nalu drove up. The two guys greeted Nalu with fist bumps.

"Hey, Nalu, sorry about your ma," they both said.

"Thanks, Kevin and Marlon," she said, her chin trembling as she looked away.

She walked behind the trailer to her mom's orchids. Big blooming specimen-size Cattleyas sat on a table and some Vandas with eight-foot-long air roots hung on hooks from the trees. These were truly some old collectors' items. Sienna hadn't expected this. She swallowed. It would be tough transporting them down the road and even tougher shipping them to Florida. Nalu looked helplessly at Sienna because she had no idea how to pack them up.

"Let's do everything else first and then we can put the orchids on top of everything, into the cracks. Let's also take this table. It's nice. And we can hang the long Vandas on the hangers in the cars."

They took the Cattleyas off the table, and Sienna carried the table over to the Jeep. Then Sienna and Nalu followed Mark into the trailer. It was a mess. Dirty dishes were piled up in the sink and on the counter, a cockroach scurried across the floor as they walked in, unwashed clothes had been thrown all over the bed, unopened mail and other paperwork was strewn across the counter and table. Palila hadn't been able to take care of everything anymore due to her illness. Nalu's cheeks turned red as she threw some old takeout containers in the trash.

"I tried to help Mom, but sometimes the water didn't even

work."

"It wasn't your or your mom's fault. It was too much for you guys to handle, Nalu. No big deal," said Sienna.

"We'll take care of it now," added Mark. "Do you have any idea where your mom had her old paperwork? I need to see if she had a rental agreement for the parking lot, and I also want to look for paperwork about your old house."

"She had a couple of binders over there on the shelf." Nalu walked back to a custom-made cabinet. Books, photo albums, binders and a few beautifully framed photos depicting Palila and Nalu in better days lined the shelves.

Sienna started cleaning up the kitchen area and washing the dishes while Nalu went through the rest of her things in the trailer. Mark sorted the mail first, then he looked through the binders. He finally found a folder with a bunch of unfiled and even unopened letters from a bank and looked inside. Jackpot. It was the foreclosure paperwork.

"Sienna, can you come over here and take a look at this?"

Sienna walked to the back of the trailer. Mark was sitting on the bed, surrounded by the paperwork.

"Look at this. It looks like she had some newspaper articles about a new law called the 'Āina Kupuna Bill that was implemented last year on Maui."

He pulled out a letter.

"In this letter she wrote to the bank mentioning that new bill, but it looks like she was blown off and told she didn't fulfill the requirements."

"It looks like they wouldn't have foreclosed on her plantation if they had taken this into consideration. She was paying outrageous taxes."

"And look at the dates. She didn't start becoming insolvent on her taxes until after this new bill was implemented."

"Do you remember Tom, the guy I met?" asked Sienna. "That's exactly what he does. He works as a lawyer for a nonprofit organization that helps locals in these situations."

Mark didn't think twice. "Please call him," he said.

Sienna called Tom and put him on speakerphone as she explained the situation.

Tom replied, "That's exactly what we do here. The 'Āina Kupuna Bill assists descendants who have held on to their family property for the past eighty years qualify for the minimum property tax rate which is $350 per year. It sounds like she was still being forced to pay thousands that she didn't have. And that's why we started this organization. Lots of kanaka are blown off by the banks and aren't insistent enough and then can't pay the crazy tax rates. Do you know how long the property has been in her family?"

"As far as I know for generations," replied Mark.

"It must have been in the family for at least eighty years. We can check that in her tax paperwork," said Tom. "Can I meet you guys tomorrow? Bring me the paperwork, and I'll make an appointment with the bank. I might be able to file an appeal to get the property back if she fulfilled the requirements."

Mark and Sienna looked at each other with big eyes. There was hope that Nalu would get her ancestors' property back out of the hands of crooked developer Joe McAllen. Sienna neatened the paperwork and put it back into the folder, sorted by date.

They took some of the photo albums and other paperwork and more of Nalu's clothes and loaded everything, including the table and the orchids, into the two cars. They'd have to take a trip to a dumpster, but then everything would be emptied.

Back at the house, Sienna helped Nalu carry the table and orchids back into the corner of the yard she had chosen and hung the Vandas into the trees. They would figure out later whether the orchids needed to go to Lani's house in Hāna or to Florida.

In the evening, they ate takeout with Josh on the beach and told him about their work emptying the trailer.

"Do you know where to dump all the garbage?" Mark asked.

"You'll have to call the Solid Waste Division. There are places you can drop it off," he replied. "But, hey, why don't you hold off a little with selling the trailer," he added jokingly. "After looking at some apartments again today, with the current real estate prices I might have to move in there."

They all laughed but knew it really wasn't funny.

Chapter 35

On Friday, after Mark finished work, Mark, Sienna, Nalu and Josh headed back to Hāna for Palila's celebration of life which was scheduled for the next day. Everything had been coming together. The trailer was emptied and sold to one of the guys who had been working the produce stand. He was also going to take over the business. For now, they decided to take Palila's orchids to Lani's house. They couldn't stay in Clark Lang's house forever, and there wasn't a better caregiver for orchids. Luana and Lani even had the agricultural stamp for their nursery and would be able to ship them whenever Nalu was ready to go to Florida.

Tom had been working on Palila's estate's premature foreclosure. It looked like they would be able to prove the bank had made a mistake, and they would get the plantation back out of Joseph McAllen's greedy hands. Nobody knew what they would do with it at this point, but it was Nalu's inheritance and belonged to her.

They were all nervous about returning to Hāna. Facing the place of her mother's death could plunge Nalu back into grief. She felt sad seeing all the places her mom had been last. However, she also felt like she was visiting her, especially at

Palila's favorite spot down by the water. The honu had returned. He felt like an old friend. Something was different about his eyes. Nalu wondered if it was her mom returning as a honu, as an 'aumakau, watching over her now.

Since Lani was taking care of the catering for the big event tomorrow, Luana and Paul had everyone over for dinner at their cottage. A celebration of life always ended in a big feast, and many friends were expected to come. Lani's place was a wreck preparing for it.

Josh was staying in Paul's and Luana's mother-in-law suite. Mark, Sienna and Nalu were staying in the guesthouse at Kōkī Beach House this time since it was bigger. Paul was excited to present a new painting, a honu in bright shades of green and gold, that he had finally completed in the past few days. Nalu was so taken by the painting that he gifted it to her, and she named it "Palila."

Yummy chicken curry from one of the trucks in town was served. Besides a few exclamations of "ono grindz" and some chewing, not much else was heard.

<hr />

The sun shone brightly the next day. It was the kind of day Palila loved and, in her better years, would've had her heading for the surf. Everyone gathered at Hāmoa Beach in casual clothes and bathing suits. The beach was crowded. It seemed like the whole island came for the celebration. Everyone wore a lei and had either a canoe, kayak or surfboard they were going to paddle out on for the ceremony.

Nalu, with a haku lei on her head, carefully carried the urn with Palila's ashes, assisted by Sienna, as they climbed into one of the large outrigger canoes with Mark, Luana and Paul. Lani, Max, Kai and Paulo climbed into the other one as the closest family and friends along with Ana, who was acting as the officiant.

Luana and Lani distributed huge amounts of plumeria and other flowers to everyone. All attendees paddled out. They surrounded the funeral boat, forming a circle, and held hands as they floated on the ocean's surface. Max held up a big pū, a conch shell, and blew it several times. The call announced the official beginning of a Hawaiian ceremony. The deep sound of the shell echoed throughout Hāmoa Beach and across the ocean. Ana chanted, giving thanks to the spirits and asking for a good afterlife for Palila.

Max played some beautiful songs on his ukulele. Everyone who could, sang along. Nalu handed Ana the urn, and Ana spread out the ashes then handed the urn back to Nalu to pour some out as well. Just as Nalu poured some ashes into the ocean with tears in her eyes, she had an idea. She whispered into Sienna's ear, "Can I keep some? I could take them to Florida and that way Mom could come with me."

Sienna looked at Nalu with tears in her eyes, then whispered into Mark's ear. For the first time, Nalu had officially said she was coming to Florida.

Mark squeezed Sienna's hand as he asked Ana, "Is that okay, Ana, for Nalu to keep some of her mom's ashes?"

"Yes, a lot of people do that to keep a memory of their loved one," said Ana. "Keep enough to fill a little square box, Nalu. I have something in mind that I can give you." She was happy

Nalu had said she was going to Florida. That was a first step in the healing process.

Everyone threw the plumeria blooms into the water. Musicians played their instruments as everyone joined in the melancholic song and sang. The sun sparkled on the calm ocean with flowers as far as the eye could reach as the canoes, outriggers and surfboards made their way back to shore. Curious beach goers watched as the group walked out of the water and continued up to Kōkī Beach House.

A juvenile honu stuck his head out of the water, watching the procession. Nalu was the only one who noticed him. She kept it to herself and winked at him. She knew she'd be back to where the honu swim.

The honu dove down and joined a group of others as they elegantly swam away.

Dear Reader,

I hope you enjoyed this story. A bit of truth, a bit of hope, a bit of fantasy and a bit of how some of us would like afterlife to be. Cancer has touched almost all of us, and I hope this story isn't too upsetting and too close to home for many of you.

Thankfully, there haven't been any recorded cases of honu poaching on Maui in a long time, and let's hope it stays that way. Maybe people have realized how important the honu are for us humans and especially the Hawaiian culture and will continue to help fight against pollution and other dangers to them such as fishing line and other sources of injuries. Please place any fishing line you find on the beach or have used while you were fishing and need to discard into the receptacles that have been set up by the rescue organizations, and volunteer in other beach clean ups if you can. It's imperative we protect our oceans.

Please remember that this story is fiction and – even in the story – no honu was actually taken or harmed.

Thank you to my mother-in-law, Lucille Van Wormer, 92 years old, who is somewhat of an elder herself and gives me a lot of inspiration for the character of Ana. She raised six kids while always working, has countless grandkids and great-grandkids, is a true matriarch and has an answer to most every health-related or life-related question. As her health is starting to decline a little, I'd say that every single one of her kids still calls her on an almost daily basis to get some type of advice or to just talk to her. She is my biggest cheerleader and knows how to keep me at task while writing and bouncing the first ideas back and forth, and I don't think I could do it without her.

My good friend Jane Harm-Barr is another rock for me. Despite her chronic health issues, she is always there to proofread everything I write and has great ideas to improve my sometimes long, nested sentences and my funny expressions, sometimes translated too directly from the German language. Jane should have been an editor!

Also, mahalo to my husband and sons who put up with me writing ten+ hours a day and my friend Kathy Penwell who has lived in Hawaii for 49 years and read this, checking the Hawaiian blurbs for spelling and correct wording and cultural sensitivity.

Last but not least mahalo to Alexzandria Braun who came up with the idea of and created the gorgeous cover as well as Emily Kline my editor.

If you liked this novel, please leave a review on Amazon, Goodreads or spread the word to friends and family. This is the only way we self-publishing authors can prevail and continue spreading the word about issues that are important to us.

Mahalo nui loa!

Thank you very much!

Birgitt Van Wormer

Huli Huli Chicken Recipe

Huli means "turn" in Hawaiian, so you basically rotate this chicken on the grill several times after marinating it in the sauce for at least a few hours. It's also a good idea to keep some of the marinade for basting. (This is one of many options and not the original Kōkī Beach recipe!)

Ingredients:

2-3 pounds of chicken (thighs work well and turn out juicier than breasts)

1 cup unsweetened pineapple juice

½ cup soy sauce

½ cup brown sugar (I use less and it doesn't seem to matter)

⅓ cup ketchup

¼ cup sherry

1 (2 inch) piece fresh ginger

3 cloves of garlic, crushed

4 green onions (chopped)

¼ teaspoon dry mustard

Combine all the ingredients in a bowl, place the sauce and the chicken pieces into a Ziploc bag and massage bag to coat the entire chicken with the marinade. Refrigerate for at least four hours.

BBQ on grill, turning the chicken and basting it with the marinade. Serve with macaroni salad and rice!

Keu a ka 'ono – bon appetit!

Acknowledgements

Finally, I'd say mahalo to the following websites and organizations from which I obtained great inspiration and information about honu, Hawaiian culture and legends:

https://campolowalu.com

https://www.danielsullivanphotography.com

https://kipahulu.org/whatwedo/mokusignage/

https://savehanacoast.org

https://www.to-hawaii.com/legends/night-marchers.php

https://atlantisadventures.com/hawaiian-legends-naupaka-the-half-flower/

https://www.holualoainn.com/the-hawaiian-honu-symbol-of-wisdom-and-good-luck/

http://mocmarineinstitute.org

Mahalo to the gracious people of the Maui Ocean Center Marine Institute for the tour of their facilities and for sharing valuable information about their work. If you ever come across a sea turtle in distress, please call the Maui Sea Turtle Stranding (and Injury) Hotline: 808-286-2549.